I wagered deep on the run of six rats to see which would catch the first fire

Surrealists and Outsiders - 2018

Edited by RW Spryszak

THRICE PUBLISHING ™
ThricePublishing.com

PO Box 725114
Roselle, IL 60172
USA

AN ACKNOWLEDGMENT

In their own way, with a word, a lead, a lasting inspiration, or a language skill desperately needed, the editor wishes to thank for all aid large and small, whether they knew they were helping or not...

María Ibarra Lorence, Rebecca Zorach, and Penelope Rosemont

The cover image is from an 1896 engraving from artist Stanley Llewellyn Wood from a book titled "Doctor Nikola, etc." It is a public domain, license-free image that has been collected and curated by The British Library

Some of the entries displayed herein as follows may, indeed, use a smaller typeface or alternative borders than the rest of the collection in order to preserve the line spacing of the original work and the intention of the writer. It is not your eyes. It is only the inconvenience of your faulty need for order.

PART ONE

THE RINGMASTER SPEAKS OF THE ARC ON FIRE

"In a sense, all outsider art is surrealist art, and we really appreciate it, and it would be interesting—we've been trying to urge a friend for years to write about the connections, because the surrealists discovered the postmaster Cheval and his work in France quite early, and they celebrated quite a few other outsider artists there."

-Penelope Rosemont

(From an interview with Rebecca Zorach that can be found at never-the-same.org.)

SURREALISM ISN'T DEAD

THE RATS HAVE FOUND PLENTY OF PINS BENEATH THE CAKES

I began this in anger on behalf of people I've never met. Like Kurt Schwitters' relationship to the Dadaists, I also have a bourgeois face and cannot directly make a claim of being among the ranks of the Surrealists. My stuff has been called a lot of things. But I've never heard it classified as Surrealist by any living practitioner. My understanding and affection for it comes because I've been lucky in my associations with artists and writers who work with the fiery gauze of Surrealism, and I confess to a personal, lifelong passion for all the forms it takes.

I knew of the current line of Surrealists. Some still living are directly connected by simple degrees of physical separation from Breton himself. But I also know others who continue to mine from the same miasmic, unconscious vein as the originals. I knew of the groups that work all over the world. Leeds. Paris. Uruguay. Stockholm. Here in the US. And so many others. All you have to do is look. There are still art shows, publications, manifestos, and adherents who simply live it. I also know of the dilution of the definition of Surrealism that seems to permeate the sad old conscious world. Part of its colloquial "demise."

This false death began with the easy portals. Dali's work turned into almost yawn-worthy icons. Magritte's work turned into dorm room posters. Those who confuse it with Fabulism or magic fantasy. Those who confuse it. A woman's house catches fire and the news reporter puts a microphone in her face and asks what it was like. She sniffles and says "It was so surreal."

No it wasn't.

I was told by a well-educated and highly degreed gentleman that Surrealism died in the 1960s. That everything that came after, calling itself Surrealism, had no contact with the original "school." Something about how everything that followed was simply cheap imitation.

I didn't know where to start with this boob. His degree. The 1960s. The "School" of Surrealism. Imitation. He wasn't even speaking a language a Surrealist would understand.

Today and for decades the physical image – painting and art and objects - has been the vanguard of Surrealism. But unless one is a student of art history or simply alive and paying attention, it can be said that few not connected to the process know that the beginnings of Surrealism came in the form of the written word. The page inhabited. Because of the preponderance of artwork and its presentation as the pinnacle of Surrealism, not many have ever read Breton's *Nadja* or the stories of Leonora Carrington. Nor are they willing to spend the time to find the seeds of the idea in the poems of Apollinaire – who named it.

--

I met Franklin Rosemont once a very long time ago. I was told his name; no one ever told him mine. He had a large beard. I think it spoke. It was in the 1970s. I can't for the life of me recall the exact circumstances. But it had something to do with the times. It's my one claim to two degrees of separation from Breton. The claim goes well with my bourgeois face, don't you think? Franklin's work for the radical labor movement and the Surrealists remains a legacy to remember.

I never met Penelope Rosemont, but it was the confluence of the above conversation with the "degreed gentleman" who declared the death of Surrealism, with my reading of an interview she gave to Rebecca Zorach that directly led to this anthology in your hands. Because in that interview, in only a somewhat passing reference – that is, not the subject of the interview itself – Penelope brought "outsider art" directly into the picture. A connection of like processes.

My two affections. Surrealism and Outsider Art. Brought under the same roof, officially, by Penelope Rosemont.

This was all I needed.

--

The idea behind this collection was to delve into the written world of Surrealism's pulse RIGHT NOW. Not the long established work that forms the foundation, so to speak. But what is being done in present time. There is a wide amount of such work that by its quantity alone proves the point that Surrealism isn't dead and, in fact, never died.

I sent out the call through groups and individuals close to the heart of it. A handful of associated spread the word. And what we've been given in return is the full range of the games - automatic writing, the genius of chance, the facets of the unconscious that pierce into the real, and (though he later broke off for his own vision) the Dadaist, anti-academic ardor of Jean Arp, who argued against what he called "impossible perfection" as an unwanted extension of mere ego.

I wanted to find material produced by women and men who wrote what they knew was there, not what was obvious, because we know for a fact that the obvious can be a sham. The appearance of freedom being the actual means of devious control. Of late, this is an everyday observation in America, certainly.

And although many publications of this nature structure a theme and send out calls for artists, poets and writers to conform to it as the basis of the work sought after – and do this with good success – I have personally never understood that. Why ask some of the world's great creatives to conform to a theme rather than give us their own full treatment from the depths of the pits they find themselves in at the moment? So, the first rule of this collection was – there is no rule.

It also should be said here, though, that among contemporary Surrealists there exists a concern for the understanding of an important distinction. In their view there is far too much kitsch being passed off under the title of "Surrealism." Too much kidnapping of the term "Surrealism" to further crass agendas of questionable merit. There is a specific meaning to the word. Surrealism, as a process and not a genre, as an idea rather than an academy, is a specific thing. And the eye's mind that understands this in a deep way should be able to discern what does and does not belong under the heading. I've tried to hold true to that distinction here.

I decided not to separate the "types" we are using. Surrealist. Outsider. You will see Outsider work (no, you don't have to be dead to be called such, I use the idea that creates a kind of *brut paradis*, naïve, straight from the soul without the false map of any academic constraint) next to the Surrealists.

This collection is divided into two parts. PART ONE, including this introduction, primarily expresses the resistance to a pseudo-surrealist poser and his sycophants registered here once and for all by an international array of Surrealists. This is followed by a round of current Surrealist thinking.

And, finally, in PART TWO, the rats tease the fire.

A NOTE ABOUT NATIONAL DESIGNATIONS

Countries hide behind national borders. They are, in reality, make believe. You can't see borders from outer space. They are all in your mind. Not real. A construct of the myth of ownership and property, and selfishness. You will, however, notice that these designations may be found beneath the name of each contributor. I am doing this to help prove my original point (above). Surrealism is alive and worldwide still. The "countries" are provided for the make-believers and the skeptics.

You will also note a preponderance of contributors from the "USA." This is in no means meant to suggest that that singular, ridiculous plutocracy located somewhere in "North America" is the international center or home or incubator of Surrealism. It most certainly is not. It is strictly a matter of how far and wide my call got out, and the responses as they related to the publishing timeline we set for this project. If we continue this series –which I have every hope of doing – it is my intention and preference to expand the roster to still more people trapped in their make believe kingdoms around the orb, until such time as we can do away with national designations altogether.

RW Spryszak
Chicago 2018

NO! TO THE RETURN OF THE TEMPLARS OF RUBBISH

On the fraudulent activities of 'Surrealism-Now'

What today is labeled as 'Art' has nothing to do with Imagination and the Marvelous and, in most cases, is no more than a fabricated rendering of the miserabilism that dominates the world. Of course, there are exceptions, those oxygenated brilliancies we seek in our quest for the gold of time, inspired marvels that will never follow the rules of academic aesthetics. What interests us most in art is the act of creating, rather than the result: as already made clear by André Breton in 1928, in his essay *Surrealism and Painting*, there is no such thing as 'surrealist art'. Painting, poetry, photography, sculpture and cinema, amongst other activities, are, for us, means of transforming our relationship with the world. Poetic inspiration is not a secondary phenomenon for us; it is essential for all authentic art. Abandoning poetic inspiration for the sake of social pressures or those of the market would result in the absurd consequence of destroying the creative spirit itself.

The total submission to conformist social codes and to the rules of the market by an association of pseudo-artists deceitfully calling itself the 'International Movement Surrealism-Now' compels us to caution all sympathizers with Surrealism against this band of swindlers and purveyors of rubbish.

Under the leadership of a certain Santiago Ribeiro, this grouping has already manifested itself, in 2014, in a collective exhibition at the historic Headquarters of the Knights Templar in the town of Condeixa, near Coimbra, Portugal.

Now, the same band, still led by Mr. Ribeiro, who has informed the media that he is "the main leader" of the "largest surrealist group in the world", with "over one hundred participants from more than twenty-five countries", and having a number of church-muralists and militarists as members, is once again exhibiting in Condeixa, an event that has been widely publicized. Here are some quotes from an interview with Santiago Ribeiro that might shed some light on the 'philosophy' of the 'Surrealism-Now' enterprise:

* Surrealism in the twenty-first century is completely different from the movement that appeared in 1924, when Breton launched his manifesto. Today's realities are completely different: today, we have

global warming, generalized capitalism and a completely different form of communicating...

* If Surrealism is to survive, it has to live in accordance with the present era...

* Surrealism according to Breton's principles is not something to which I would like to belong.

* My own painting has an ancient atmosphere of crucifixion...

* Something that does not exist is what I call 'surreal'...

* There are places in our country of such beauty that we take the opportunity to talk about their cultural and historical richness while at the same time promoting our art...

We reply to this opportunist Ribeiro and his 'Surrealism-Now' gang: DAMN YOU ALL!

The aspirations of true Surrealism are elsewhere: the advent of a new civilization where banal reality will be transformed into a marvelous surreality. We despise your ridiculous, demagogic and cacophonic manifestations that falsify Surrealism's ambitions and aspirations and that attempt to take commercial advantage from a fraudulent activity.

This declaration has been signed by the surrealists:

Xoan Abeleira; Jaime Alfaro; Alberto Assumpção; Melatonino Beal; Magdalena Benavente; Jan Bervoets; Verónica Cabanillas; Miguel de Carvalho; Eugenio Castro; José Miguel Pérez Corrales; Daniel Cotrina; David Coulter; Kenneth Cox; Célia Cymbalista; Luke Dominey; Guy Ducornet; Kathleen Fox; Victor Fuentes Marambio; Tono Galán; Javier Gálvez; Guy Girard et les autres membres du Groupe de Paris du Mouvement Surréaliste; Xesús González Gómez; Allan Graubard; Vicente Gutiérrez Escudero; Janice Hathaway; Beatriz Hausner; Mazo Heck; Rodrigo Hernández Piceros; Dale Houston; Bill Howe; Karl Howeth; Joseph Jablonski; Bruno Jacobs; Alex Januário; Patrick Lepetit; Sergio Lima; Rik Lina; Léo Litha; Michael Löwy; Alexandre Magno; Lurdes Martínez; Armando McMurray; Richard Misiano-Genovese, Luiz Morgadinho; David Nadeau; Peter Overton; Jean-

Pierre Paraggio; Gregorio Paredes; Nelson de Paula; Seixas Peixoto; Pierre Petiot; Pedro Prata; Carlos Rangel; Raman Rao; Alejandro Rejon Huchin; John Richardson; José Manuel Rojo; Penelope Rosemont; Enrique de Santiago; Gregg Simpson; Dan Stanciu; Ludovic Tac; Jonathan Tarry; Laurens Vancrevel; Rodrigo Verdugo Pizarro; Cristina Vouga; Claudia Vila; Her de Vries; Richard Waara; Zazie Evi Möchel; being members of the following surrealist groups: Cabo Mondego Section of Portuguese Surrealism; Grupo Surrealista de Madrid; Leeds Surrealist Group; Groupe de Paris du Mouvement Surréaliste; Chicago Surrealist Group; Xalundes/Grupo Surrealista Galego; Brumes Blondes, Holland; Grupo Surrealista Derrame (Chile); Grupo Surrealista de São Paulo; Grupo Surrealista Agharta (Chile); Grupo DeCollage (São Paulo); Groupe le Vertèbre et le Rossignol; Peculiar Mormyrid Group; joined by independent surrealists and sympathizers; acting together in the service of the International Movement of Surrealism.

January 19, 2018

DO RIBEIRO AO ESGOTO / DU RUISSEAU À L'ÉGOUT

On connaît le sort que le langage vulgaire, si prisé de la valetaille médiatique et complaisamment répercuté par elle, a réservé au surréalisme : il aurait été fondé par un pape, nommé André Breton et il désignerait un gag littéraire et artistique puisant ses effets dans l'insolite et les aberrations, incitant à la provocation gratuite et au geste absurde. Ces sottises ont été si souvent rabâchées que les dénoncer toutes à chaque fois qu'elles sont émises représenterait un véritable travail de Sisyphe ; ce qui fait que, la plupart du temps elles ne suscitent plus chez nous qu'un haussement d'épaules fatigué. Mais aujourd'hui le surréalisme risque de se voir attribuer une acception nouvelle : celle de pure et simple escroquerie. Et là, nous nous permettons de nous fâcher.

Depuis quelques années, en effet, un certain Santiago Ribeiro, né à Coimbra en 1964, expose son inoffensive barbouille un peu partout dans le monde. Comme ses tableaux exhibent un vague univers fantastique, il a cru bon de se proclamer peintre surréaliste. Démarche partagée du reste par un certain nombre d'autres rapins qui n'ont toujours pas compris que, dans la mesure où le surréalisme n'est pas une école artistique ni littéraire, mais une attitude de l'esprit, il ne saurait y avoir de peinture surréaliste, et seulement un usage surréaliste de la peinture. Mais passons. Ce qui est infiniment plus grave, c'est que le sieur Ribeiro fait du surréalisme une marque de fabrique, labellisée sous l'étiquette *Surrealism now* qui, de juillet à décembre 2017, s'étalait, comble de l'ignominie, en bandeau publicitaire sur les écrans géants de Times Square à New York. Car tel est bien là l'inacceptable. Même Dali, dont les excentricités n'ont pas peu contribué à l'assimilation vulgaire du surréalisme à la bizarrerie loufoque, mais qui ne manquait pas de génie, n'était pas allé aussi loin dans le détournement du sens. Son alter ego, Avida Dollars, au moins, travaillait pour lui seul et ne prétendait pas organiser un mouvement planétaire entraînant plus d'une centaine de participants. D'autant que le promoteur de ce mouvement renie explicitement tous les fondements éthiques et critiques du surréalisme : il se réclame ouvertement de la religion (« Mon art à moi baigne dans la vieille atmosphère de la crucifixion »), il n'hésite pas à faire appel à des peintres d'église, à des militaristes déclarés, et enfin il ne cache en rien qu'il agit en opposition au fondateur même du mouvement dont il se réclame bruyamment (« Un surréalisme basé sur les principes de Breton ne présente pour moi aucun intérêt dans les circonstances actuelles »). Alors que c'est André Breton qui, avec le *Manifeste* de 1924 et les textes automatiques comme *Les Champs magnétiques* et *Poisson soluble,* a donné tout son contenu au terme surréalisme, c'est faire preuve d'une singulière outrecuidance que prétendre en redéfinir aujourd'hui d'une façon si grotesque et perfide les fondements et les objectifs. Le prétendu *Surrealism now* n'est ni surréaliste ni actuel, c'est une authentique escroquerie intellectuelle comme il s'en est monté à toutes les époques.

Paris, le 25 janvier 2018

Pour le Groupe surréaliste :

Élise Aru, Michèle Bachelet, Anny Bonnin, Massimo Borghese, Claude-Lucien Cauët, Hervé Delabarre, Alfredo Fernandes, Joël Gayraud, Guy Girard, Michael Löwy, Pierre-André Sauvageot, Bertrand Schmitt, Sylvain Tanquerel, Virginia Tentindo, Michel Zimbacca.

DO RIBEIRO AO ESGOTO / FROM STREAM TO SEWER

We know the fate that the vulgar language so prized by media lackeys, and complacently echoed by them, has reserved for Surrealism: it was founded by a 'pope' named André Breton, and it designates a literary and artistic gag resulting in bizarre aberrations, inciting gratuitous provocations and absurd gestures. These stupidities have been rehashed so often that denouncing them every time they are issued would be a veritable labour of Sisyphus; meaning that, most of the time, they do not provoke more than a tired shrug of our shoulders. But today, Surrealism is at risk of being assigned a new meaning: that of a scam, pure and simple. And here we'll allow ourselves to become angry.

For a number of years, a certain Santiago Ribeiro, born in Coimbra in 1964, has exhibited his harmless daubs the world over. Since his paintings represent a vague fantasy universe, he thought it best to proclaim himself a surrealist painter. This approach is shared by a number of other daubers who have not yet understood that, insofar as Surrealism is neither an artistic nor a literary school, but an attitude of the mind, there cannot be such a thing as 'surrealist painting', only a surrealist use of painting. But let's move on. What is infinitely more serious is that Mr. Ribeiro turns Surrealism into a trademark, registered under the label *Surrealism Now,* which—the height of ignominy—spreads its advertising banner across the giant screens of Times Square in New York City from July to December 2017. This is truly unacceptable. Even Dali, not lacking genius, whose eccentricities contributed not a little to the vulgar association of Surrealism with zany weirdness, never went so far in the misappropriation of its meaning. His alter ego, Avida Dollars, at least worked for himself alone and did not claim to organize a global movement involving more than a hundred participants. Especially since the promoter of this movement explicitly rejects all of Surrealism's ethical and critical foundations: he openly upholds religion ("My art is bathed in the old atmosphere of crucifixion"), does not hesitate to appeal to church painters, to declared militarists, and makes no secret of acting in opposition to the founder of the very movement to which he loudly claims to belong ("A Surrealism based on Breton's principles does not present any interest to me in the current circumstances"). As it was André Breton who, with the *Manifesto* of 1924 and automatic texts such as *Magnetic Fields* and *Soluble Fish,* filled the term Surrealism with content, it demonstrates a singular presumption to purport to redefine today Surrealism's founding principles and objectives in such a grotesque and deceitful way. *Surrealism Now*, his so-called Surrealism for our time, is neither surreal nor current; it is a veritable intellectual swindle such as is practiced in every age.

Paris, 25th January, 2018
(translated by Kenneth Cox)

For the surrealist group:
Élise Aru, Michèle Bachelet, Anny Bonnin, Massimo Borghese, Claude-Lucien Cauët, Hervé Delabarre, Alfredo Fernandes, Joël Gayraud, Guy Girard, Michael Löwy, Pierre-André Sauvageot, Bertrand Schmitt, SylvainTanquerel, Virginia Tentindo, Michel Zimbacca.

DAVID NADEAU
Canada

MYSTERIOUS BLACKSMITHS

An article by the Surrealist poet Jean-Pierre Lassalle entitled "André Breton et la franc-maçonnerie 1" revealed to lay people the existence of a core of active Freemasons, from the fifties, inside and near the Surrealist group of Paris. These individuals were linked to a lodge of the Grande Loge de France, founded in 1901 and bearing the distinctive title of Thebah ("The Arch" in Hebrew). At the time, the Grande Loge showed some fundamental divergences with the Grand Orient de France, more interested in political and social involvement, especially on the issue of secularism and modern humanism. The Grand Loge of France, another important branch of Freemasonry in this country, represented then the more traditional and esoteric side. It practices the Old and Accepted Scottish Rite 2.

According to Jean-Pierre Lassalle, the recruitment of Thebah lodge "was selective and there were many original spirits, both tradition-oriented and open to innovators 3". The esoteric writer René Guénon was initiated there in 1912, twelve years before, moreover, he declined the invitation to join the nascent surrealist group...

"In a few years," says Lassalle, "Thebah Lodge gathered several Surrealists among whom [René] Alleau, Élie-Charles Flamand, Bernard Roger, Guy-René Doumayrou, Roger Van Hecke, Jean Palou 4." The name of Henry Hunwald, doctor and alchemist close to Maryse Zimbacca, must also be quoted. We will see later that almost all practice alchemy. Among these individuals, René Alleau, Guy-René Doumayrou and Bernard Roger continued to maintain relations with the Surrealists of Paris. In the petition "Le grimoire sans la formule", launched in 2003 by Fabrice Pascaud, following threats to sell the contents of the former studio of André Breton, we find the signatures of Lassalle, Flamand, Doumayrou and Alleau, alongside those of Emmanuel Fenet and Michael Lowy, two members of the Paris Group of the Surrealist Movement.

"The absent of herself
Escapes from your fallen parks

She pretends to submit our hours
And renew the ancestral trappings
On the passage of false losers
Who come to dig the darkness with their laughter
While Gérard dances with the Dioscuri
On the lawn of a childish serenity
Forever preserved from your reminiscences
Of the destructive deities of the desert 5"

Among the Surrealist writers affiliated with the Thebah Lodge, some discretely claim an initiatory tradition represented by the figure of certain blacksmith gods of pre-Hellenic Antiquity. The alchemist and historian René Alleau, in his book Aspects de l'Alchimie traditionnelle, mentions five different figures of mythical blacksmiths. The Dactyls work iron, and are reputed jugglers and magicians. They also practice medicine. According to Strabo, Curetes and Corybantes are derived from Dactyls; their dances represent "the revolutions of the planets". The Telchines of Rhodes executed the first bronze statues in the image of the gods. The Cabires, which René Alleau presents more in his study than the other groups of blacksmiths, forge the sickle of Kronos. The author of Aspects de l'alchimie traditionnelle groups these different figures of mythical blacksmiths under the term "fire theurgists". They are the guardian geniuses of underground fire and fabulous transformations specific to the practice of alchemy.

THE INITIATION TO THE MYSTERIES OF SAMOTHRACE

The sons of Vulcan, or of Jupiter and Prosperine, the Cabires populate the iron mines of Samothrace, named Island of Sickle, since it was there that Vulcan forged the weapon of Ceres and Titans. These blacksmiths, frequently represented with hammer and pincers, work the metals that grow under the Earth. They are also geniuses of fertility. The etymology of their name goes back to the Greek "kaio", which means to ignite, to consume.

A Medal of Trajan shows a Cabire, the head crowned with a pointed cap 6; in one hand he holds a branch of cypresses and on the other a square. His coat is spread over his shoulders and he is wearing cothurni. Cabiric cults bear the imprint of fertility rites common to Proto-Hittites and Asianics, to which were added later Egyptian, Cretan and Phoenician influences. Religious mysteries were instituted in Samothrace, which involved the practice of sacred metallurgy, a "theurgy by fire". The presence of the hammer, pincers and sickle as symbolic attributes associated with these mysteries indicates the superposition of metallurgical rites to older agrarian rites. According to Alleau, these rituals "were accompanied by libations and propitiatory sacrifices and were made at astrologically determined times according to complex calculations 7".

The Cabires also had a sanctuary at Lemnos, where they were called Carcines and Sintians, and another at Thebes. Cabiric religion became one of the most important in ancient Italy. It spread throughout the Roman Empire, and even in the Celtic countries (on this subject, see the chronicles of Strabo). Several glorious figures of Greek Antiquity, heroes and philosophers, have received initiation on the Island of Samothrace: Orpheus, Hercules, Ulysses, Pythagoras, Aeneas, Jason and the Argonauts. The Castor and Pollux twins, Pelasgian heroes known as the Dioscuri, will be presented later. The initiation of the neophyte involved a series of frightening trials, at the end of which he donned magnificent clothes, and sat on "a throne lit up with a thousand lights. He was given an olive crown on his forehead, a purple belt around his kidneys, and the other initiates performed symbolic dances under his eyes. 8" The scenes, depicted on several Etruscan mirrors, illustrate the ritual scheme of death and rebirth; for example, the one where the youngest Cabire is fatally beaten by his three brothers.

CABIRISM AND ALCHEMY ACCORDING TO RENÉ ALLEAU

For René Alleau, alchemy, like all traditional sciences, is based on a metaphysical system of thought:

"Although positive, experimental and concrete, alchemy borrows its principles from the traditional metaphysics of which it represents one of the applications to the formal domain as well as to the relations of form and light. "

He posits the hypothesis of the influence of the mysteries of blacksmiths on the development of alchemy, which he proposes to study, in the light of the metaphysical system on which the initiation to the mysteries of Cabires of Samothrace was based.

"I relied on the study of cabirism and the mysteries of Samothrace, for it seemed natural to me that mysteries of blacksmiths and metallurgists might have contributed in part to a later alchemical tradition which was doubtless linked to the priesthood and to craft. Unfortunately, the state of work on cabirism is far from allowing us to present certain data. Our hypothesis about the cabiric triad thus claims to be nothing more than a possible elucidation of some aspects of the alchemical theories.9"

In 1957, four years after the publication of Aspects de l'alchimie traditionnelle, André Breton risks an astonishing rapprochement in his voluminous essay on L'Art magique, written in collaboration with Gérard Legrand:

"The means put by Surrealism at the disposal of the imaginary activity require in return an exemplary moral commitment. Suffice it to say that Surrealism is not the master of it, and that this is a real pact with the unknown and the unmeasured, a pact whose terms can vary from one mind to another, but none the less comparable to the oath of the initiates of Samothrace not to reveal the mysteries of the Cabires, and even better to the famous pact with the devil of the medieval wizards - except that here it is about to never sell one's soul to God or to the men.10"

In addition, René Alleau responds at length to the questionnaire that completes Breton and Legrand's book. Already, some twenty years before the publication of the book of Alleau, Antonin Artaud evokes the gods of Samothrace, during a conference in Mexico, where he shared his experience of Surrealism:

"In order to reach the secret of things, surrealism has opened a path. As for the unknown god of the Cabire's Mysteries, as for the Ain-Souph, the animated hole of the abysses in Kabbalah, for the Nothing, the Void, the Non-being of the ancient Brahms and the Vedas, we can say of surrealism what it is not, but for saying what it is, one needs to use approximations and images, and surrealism is a movement clad in images. It resurrects, by a sort of incantation in the void, the spirit of ancient allegories 11."

According to the scholiast of Apollonius of Rhodes, the historian Mnaseas has made known the names associated with the cabiric triad of Samothrace: Axieros, Axiokersos and Axiokersa.

To these gods complements a subordinate god, called Cadmilos. René Alleau draws on an etymological analysis of these names to deduce a system of metaphysics of numbers, based on the symbols of the cross and the triangle. This system represents, in a synthetic way, the occult relationships between the initiate, the Sky and the Earth, the Sun and the Moon. The Cabiric triad hides another, made up of Hermes, Helios and the couple Hephaestus-Aphrodite. A marble, said of the Duchess of Chablais, preserved in the Vatican museum, represents a triangular Hermes. On this monument dedicated to the cabiric cult of Samothrace, is represented the sacred couple, formed of Dionysus-Hades and Persephone. Hermes, among them, is again a mediator. Thus, thanks to the intermediary of the sacred metallurgist, Heaven and Earth, the Sun and the Moon, are united. The ritual thus ensures the harmony of the cosmic forces.

The terms of the cabiric triad can be found in one of the postcards that Jean-Pierre Lassalle addressed to himself in 1959. These postcards were designed for the filling of the collective Alert Box (Lascivious Missives), a surrealist object created by Mimi Parent and Marcel Duchamp, on the occasion of the big EROS collective exhibition. In one of these Lascivious Missives, conceived by the poet as the word of a lover, there is a veiled allusion to the most famous monument associated with the cabiric mysteries, the *Nikè*:

"Honey, Axieros! Axiokersos! Axiokersa!
Victory robs me of race
Forever Viviane »

CABIRISM IN THE MIDDLE AGES ACCORDING TO RENÉ ALLEAU

During the Ancien Regime, the Courtyard of the Miracles of Paris, this "large muddy, irregular dead-end, which is not paved 12", was situated at the last extremities of the city. It was inhabited by the poor, as well as the artists and traveling mountebanks who came to fetch from the king and the nobles. It was obviously the den of several criminal groups. All these people form a Kingdom qualified as argotique, with its own laws, its officers, and its States-General of the Corporation of the Beggars who elect the King every year. They all spoke a peculiar language, the argot, taught and reformed by the College of the Archi-Suppôts,

25

which was composed of students and priests, described as "debauched"13 by the seventeenth-century historian Henri Sauval. The king of the Kingdom, supreme chief of the corporation of the beggars, is named Grand Coësre, and he was recognizable by his royal habits, composed of "thousand rapetaceous rags, variegated with a thousand colors". He was first the leader of a pagan and telluric religion that Rene Alleau, in Aspects de l'alchimie traditionnelle, relates to the mythical blacksmiths of Samothrace, that is to say to "currents of ancient beliefs that Roman Catholicism have never succeeded in drying up or totally diverting". If these mysterious connections are unexpected from a qualified historian, they are in line with the alchemical interpretations of different aspects of European medieval culture found in Fulcanelli's books. Societies responsible for organizing certain major popular festivals, the guilds of builders as well as the orders of chivalry, would have done esoteric works, linked to alchemy:

"All the Initiates spoke in argot, the mobsters of the Court of Miracles, - headed by the poet Villon – as well as the Frimasons, Freemasons of the Middle Ages, members of the lodge of God, who edified the argotique masterpieces we admire today. Themselves, these builder sailors, knew the road to the garden of the Hesperides ...

Even today, the humble, the miserable, the despised, the rebellious ones, avid of freedom and independence, the proscribed, the wanderers and the nomads speak the argot, this cursed dialect, banished by the high society, by the nobility (who are really so little noble), the well-fed and self-satisfied bourgeois, luxuriating in the ermine of their ignorance and fatuity. The argot remains the language of a minority of individuals living outside accepted laws, conventions, usages, protocol, to which we apply the epithet of bums, that is to say, seers, and that even more expressive, of Sons or Children of the sun. "

THE PELASGIANS ACCORDING TO FULCANELLI

The Pelasgians are at the origin of the alchemical tradition to which Fulcanelli claims to be affiliated and of the esoteric language that conveys its teaching: the language of the birds, also called phonetic cabal. Several ancient chroniclers claim that before the arrival of the Greeks, the country was peopled with pelasgic colonies. These prehellenic populations would have erected the monuments formed by polyhedral blocks and the so-called cyclopean or pelasgic walls that one encounters in Great Britain, France, Italy, Greece, and the very depths of Spain. The first kings of Athens would have been Pelasgians.

According to the author of Les Demeures Philosophales, the language of the birds is a "phonetic idiom based solely on assonance. It does not take the spelling into account". It would be at the origin of all languages. The alchemist finds the secret of this initiatory language, whose mastery allows him to read the hermetic texts and images. For Fulcanelli, the language of the birds, or phonetic cabal, "in spite of the importance and the truth of its expression, is in fact of Greek origin and genius". According to this author, the mother tongue to which the alchemists borrow their terms is archaic Greek, composed mainly of Aeolian and Dorian dialects:

"The cabal contains and preserves most of the language of the Pelasgians, a language deformed in primitive Greek, but not destroyed ; mother tongue of Western idioms, and particularly of French, whose pelasgic origin is incontestable; an admirable language, which it suffices to know a few smatterings to easily rediscover, in the various European dialects, the real meaning, alterated by time and by the migrations of peoples, from the original language.14"

Fulcanelli takes a position in the philological debate on the origins of the French langage, by opposing the defenders of the neo-Latinist thesis, of which, citing JL Dartois, he denounces the inanity: "our language ... was Greek ... Roman domination in Gaul had only covered it with a slight layer of Latin without in any way altering its genius". The unknown alchemist defends the thesis of the "kinship and not the filiation of so-called neo-Latin languages". According to Fulcanelli, this Greek philological fact "proves, without question, that the tribes that came to populate the west of Europe were pelasgic colonies".

The Pelasgian origin of the mysteries of Samothrace is recounted by Herodotus, in his chronicles of the conquest of Egypt by Cambyse II, son of Cyrus 15.

DIOSCURES

The architects and esoterists Guy-René Doumayrou and Bernard Roger follow the path of the twin brothers Castor and Pollux, these marine gods who, in the form of two stars16, guide the Argonauts in their navigation in search of the Golden Fleece. These Dioscuri are thought to be the sons of Zeus and Leda. Their attributes are the white horse, the star and the spear. The Etruscan mirrors show the two brothers around their companion, who is represented in the form of a beautiful goddess or that of the crescent moon. In an article titled "Le Jour de l'Étoile", Bernard Roger reproduces images of some of these fascinating ritual objects. Priests of Samothrace, Castor and Pollux are sometimes identified with the Cabires, of which they wear the distinctive emblem: the pileus. Gilbert Durand, in Structures anthropologiques de l'imaginaire, notes this:

"Dioscuri and Cabires wear the pointed cap - the pileus- which was transmitted as a secret emblem in certain religious mysteries and became the cap of Attis, of Mithra, then the gnomes, the goblins and the seven dwarfs of the legend.17"

In Géographie Sidérale, Guy-René Doumayrou expresses the same idea that goblins and gnomes ensure the survival of "old telluric deities" in rural beliefs. Herodotus already asserts that Cabires are pot-bellied and deformed dwarves18.

The Etruscan mirrors reproduced by Bernard Roger in "Le Jour de l'Étoile" depict different stages of the initiatory myth of the Dioscuri; "Alternatively, according to the myth, one of the brothers came back to life while the other died". In the same vein, Guy-René Doumayrou explains that one of the twins is mortal while the other is immortal.

With regard to the representations of the Dioscuri, Roger notes that their frequency as well as the silence of the writers of Antiquity on the meaning that can be attributed to them "seem to indicate that these are symbols situated outside the official mythological currents".

The triad formed by the Dioscuri and the goddess would be "the basis of an ancient tradition" whose aim, "as far as man is concerned", is his liberation from the laws and conventions that ensure the social order;

"Great traditional tree in which the sap of the word circulates, whose roots are lost in the stars and whose numerous branches, directed towards the earth, each bear among its fruits the red cap of the **freedman**."

---

1 Histoires littéraires, issue 1, january 2000.

2 The Old and Accepted Scottish Rite is one of the most widespread Masonic rites in the world. It was founded in 1801 in Charleston, United States, under the leadership of John Mitchell and Frederic Dalcho. The organization of the ritual ceremonies specific to the different degrees of initiation is codified on the basis of the Great Constitutions of 1786.

3 "André Breton et la franc-maçonnerie", p.89.

4 Ibidem.

5 Excerpt from "Hors d'atteinte", by Élie-Charles Flamand, in Jouvence d'un soleil terminal, 1979.

6 Their pointed cap, the pileus, is sometimes surmounted by a star.

7 Aspects de l'alchimie traditionnelle, p.66.

8 P. Commelin, Mythologie grecque et romaine, p.201-203.

9 Aspects de l'alchimie traditionnelle, p.40

10 André Breton and Gérard Legrand, L'Art magique, p.251

11 "Surréalisme et révolution", in Messages révolutionnaires

12 Henri Sauval. Quoted in Lazare Sainéan, Les sources de l'argot ancien, Paris, H. et E. Champion, 1912, p.317.

13 Ibidem.

14 Les Demeures philosophales, Tome II, p.264.

15 Herodotus II, 51. Books I to IV of Herodotus are devoted to the development of the Persian Empire.

16 The constellation Gemini owes its name to Castor and Pollux, who are the two most brilliant stars.

17 Structures anthropologiques de l'imaginaire, p.226. On this question, Gilbert Durand refers to the work of Carl Gustav Jung entitled Metamorphoses and symbols of the libido. Philippe Audoin, in a prose poem inspired by the paintings of Gabriel Der Kevorkian, explores the same symbolic constellation: "Changed into gnomes, the old gods turned green-veronese, purple-bishop. Their contortions surround large, dull beaches where the profile of a new wisdom is outlined." This text by Philippe Audoin,

entitled "Gabriel Der Kevorkian ou la mécanique trans-rationnelle", immediately follows "Le Jour de l'Étoile" by Bernard Roger, in the issue 7 of the surrealist magazine L'Archibras. In a study devoted to the work of the writer Maurice Fourré, published in this same issue, Audoin quotes the following passage from an alchemical poem entitled "L'Échafaud d'Émeraude": "A cone of darkness buries the sulphurous night shading with black lace up to the witch waters the emerald table of the vegetable joy where the Initiator Metallurgist prowls"
18 Herodotus, III, 37.

LAURA WINTON
USA

ECRITURE FEMININE AND WOMEN'S TRANSGRESSIVE WRITING

A Manifesto, a poem,
a performance piece, and
an academic article

Three French Theorists walk into a lecture hall..
*(****Michel Foucault*** *picks things out of the trashbin of literary history.*
Voila! Stephen King's Parking Tickets
Voila! Nietzsche's Laundry List
Voila! Hemingway's hunting license
Voila! Shakespeare's supposed (typed) manuscript of his
complete works
Barthes says L'auter est mort! Vive le lecteur! But who is
speaking?
Foucault answers What does it matter who is speaking!?
Enter **Cixous:**   Of course it matters, you patriarchal
windbags. The author isn't dead, She's right here!"
"Why is that men on the left cannot see their own blind spots?
You go on all day about the oppressors and post-colonial this
and post-structural that but then you deny us our voices when
it suits you, when you don't feel the need for an author.
"Who makes me write, moan, sing, dance? Who gives me the
body that is never afraid of fear? Who writes me? . . . When I
have finished writing, when we have returned to the air of the
song that we are, the body of texts that we will have made for
ourselves will become one of its names among so many
others. In the beginning, there can be only dying, the abyss,
the first laugh"

Prologue: What is writing?

What is writing? Writing is   everything. Writing is
communication, imagination, learning, history, memory, language, there is
nothing outside the text says Derrida, and I believe it and I don't.

An attempted poetic interlude

Stream-of-Consciousness Internal Dialogue

Writing is all the knowledge and creativity and creation and evolution and revolution and punk rock and heavy metal music and hymns and poems and treatises and manifestos and novels and academic articles and everything that we have learned and try to learn and strive to learn and

know and catalogue and categorize and put into boxes marked kingdom phylum genre order class Marxist proletariat species human and text and chora and Oedipus and his daddy Freud and his Mama Jocasta and Hamlet and Cleopatra the queen and the movie the woman(en) and the myth(s). How can you not be self-conscious with the weight of all that history upon you and all that knowledge and that was only half a paragraph?

There *is* something outside the text. Unnamable feelings and joy and wild ecstatic movement and birds songs but the minute we identify it as anything at all, it moves inside the textual fence as it moves into consciousness from unconsciousness and there it sits until it becomes text and writing.

What's the use of the text? If we can't get outside of the text anymore,

    then that makes the text   a kind of . . . ideology since Zizek's theory tell us

that it is impossible to get outside of our own ideologies, outside of our own heads, outside of   the text.   Stupid   Derrida. I hate it when he's right (write).

Death of the Author: God and Mother, a Parable

In the Judeo-Christian tradition, the text, the word, is sacred. We cannot seem to get out of the tradition. For all of their post-modernism and the agnosticism that frequently comes with that, Barthes (and Derrida) also come out of a French tradition which was very very Catholic. Thus, I am going to make the story of the death of the author, male and female, into a comparative parable.

In Christianity, Jesus (the author) must die and be resurrected so that believers (readers) can have safe passage to heaven (the text). This is the male-centered conception of the author as the all-knowing keeper of the text and of meaning. And in fact, Barthes speaks of "the 'message' of the Author-God"i and says that "to refuse to fix its meaning is, in the end, to refuse God and his hypostases – reason, science, law"ii.

Women, however, have historically had a different relationship to birth and death, with many medieval women dying in childbirth. In this model, the woman (author) dies so that her child (the reader) may be born, but that child will be orphaned, with no one to guide her through life (the text). There is a "death/not death," a voluntary withdrawal that happens here that can be seen as Cixous' metaphor for the author. Cixous also talks about the (female) author as continuing "to have what she has eternally, to not lose having, to be pregnant with having is . . . the text, already in the child, in the woman . . .iii" The woman is birthing the text, bringing it into being, and like giving birth, some of herself with leave her along with the text. But that text will not necessitate a death for the author. If the reader is a co-creator in meaning, as with Barthes, the author-mother will do so in conjunction with, not opposed to, the reader and the text.

Gender and Genre

All of this brings me back to Amy Shuman's "Gender and Genre," about a possible "rejection" or at least radical rethinking of academic work and what it means to be academic, what it means for women who have traditionally done "expressive" writing – short stories and fiction, storytelling, to rethink and remake what constitutes academic writing. Is it necessarily less rigorous? What potential do we have to remake academic writing and not have it devalued, like so many things in culture become once they are associated with women and with women's work? Is rigor always to be male-defined? Must we adhere to traditionally "male" academic standards that we had no role in setting, but must maintain, nonetheless? And if we choose to change those standards or to not uphold and maintain those standards any more, will our own work be less valid? What would the new standards look like?

Right away on the first page of the article she talks "how people negotiate the categories that are imposed upon them"iv. Many of the restrictions of academic writing predate women's mass entrance into the academy and represent patriarchal categories of what "counts" as academic writing, what "counts" as academic publishing, etc. I have underlined at least half of the first page in the book because it says so much that I have come to love and agree with.

Theories of gender and genre converge in their exploration of the problems of classification and the disruption of boundaries. Genre is often gendered . . . . Gender scholarship questions how cultural categories are reproduced and under what conditions women are complicit with or resistant to the reproduction of conventions.v

Shuman continues, talking about the way that "genre classification systems could represent the values of a culturevi", and the way that "genre systems are as much about disputes, maintenance, and shifting of boundariesvii". Thus, it is no wonder that feminists coming to academic would question those kinds of boundaries.

Sol LeWitt's *Sentences on Conceptualism* question the use of rationality in art, and by extension writing, since in conceptualist art the link between the writing and theorizing and the actual making of art is dissolved. For LeWitt, "Conceptual artists are mystics rather than rationalists. They leap to conclusions that logic cannot reach." The first four sentences are about the connection (or not) of rationality with art:

1. Rational judgments repeat rational judgments.
2. Irrational judgments lead to new experience.
3. Formal art is essentially rational.
4. Irrational thoughts should be followed absolutely and logically.viii

Since women have been traditionally associated with irrationality, it seems that avant-garde art, at least by LeWitt's definition, would inherently be a feminine realm.ix   Cixous carries it farther, saying that she "has no right to write within your logic: nowhere to write from." Because she is a woman, she has "no fatherland, no legitimate history. No certainties, no property.x" With no "fatherland," no history or tradition, a woman has no "genre," she feels an allegiance to. It is all up for grabs for her to make her own history, her own traditions. And hence, her own, if illegitimate (in the eyes of men), genres.

The Liberation of the Imagination:
From "Feminine Writing" to Revolutionary Poetry

In the introduction to *Feminist Critique of Language,* editor Deborah Cameron cites a quote by Shoshona Feldman on language that particularly resonates with me and my work on poetry, language and liberation.

The challenge facing women today is nothing less than to reinvent language . . . to speak   not only against but outside the structure . . . to establish a discourse the status of which   would no longer be defined by the phallacy of male meaning.xi

Cameron elaborates further upon Feldman's idea, discussing briefly the work of French Feminists such as Luce Irigaray and Helene Cixous and a search for a "feminine writing" and "women's language." Cameron also raises the other side of the debate, citing Elaine Showalter's position that the issue for women is not so much a male-based "prisonhouse of language," as Frederic Jameson says. The very fact of access and entitlement for women to speak is not the inadequacy of language, or as Judith Butler would point to, the way in which language performs, enacts, speaks into being our condition.xii Others reject an essentialist strain that says that women *need* different language than men to express their lives, their realities, their psyches, their thoughts, etc.

To me the core issue here is that *all* marginalized, disempowered people, need access to a language of *imagination*. Not a replacement language per se, but a *paralanguage*, a language that works, functions on a completely different level than the ordinary, the quotidian, the banal, the mundane, and (consequently) the hegemonic uses of language. The language as it is now practiced, even if it is not *inherently* structured to protect and maintain power, it has certainly been subverted to that use, propagated in contemporary life, by the constant onslaught of mainstream media—advertising, news, the normative values promoted by almost all television programming and many movies. In insidious ways we are constantly being told what to believe, what to buy, how to act, how to be moral, how to be patriotic, how to look a certain way, how to fit in and belong in American society, etc. etc. How is one to rethink the world, remake the world, the government, the neighborhood, the culture, the communities we come from and live in, our own very daily existence, among the onslaught of images that perpetuate someone else's vision and serve up to us only the world as we already (think) we know it?

To   remake languageto find   new
  creative   imagistic practicesof language
is to make   resistance   possible to move us
      toward our vision   to have visions
     never   before   possible

I am talking here about a language that speaks outside of the dominant discourse, whether racialized, patriarchal, class-based, etc., an un-discourses or non-discourse, a paradiscourse, that brings with it the chance to step outside, run alongside, that does not attempt to use the tools of power that already exist, but to forge new tools that could create new structures, new edifices not previously imagined. The techne, the tool, in many ways prescribes what can be built. We know that with new technology new ways of thinking emerge. So why would we not want new mental and imaginative linguistic tools of our own? As Sol LeWitt says, "rational thoughts repeat rational thoughts." The way we think perpetuates itself, we continue to think only in the ways we've always thought. I'm not looking then for a feminine language per se, except insofar as it might offer a resistive language, a paralanguage that we can frolic in and search for something unknown, a Dada language a non-sense that leads to sense a zaum a de-formed formalism that will birth new forms.

What Do Women Want?

We want to be on the   c u t t
                                        i n g
                                             e
                                              d
                                               g
                                                e
           of literature,   to operate

(within)(outside of)   the m   a   r   g   i   n   s.
              (That is where we reside anyway.)
           We are used to working within that area
                        and we are
                        good   at   it.

    We have gotten so used to it that we are not actually considered avant-garde. It comes very naturally to us.   This is what Cixous is talking about when she speaks (or writes) of the *ecriture feminine*. If we are actually paying attention to how we function within society, even at this stage, even in 2016, we have to admit to ourselves that our involvement in culture and politics is still very radical and we operate, when we are being honest with ourselves, oppositionally.

              To be a woman writer or artist
           is to be   truly
                        and inherently
           avant-garde
                        whether
                        (you know it or not)   *(you call yourself*
              that or not).

The Revolutionary Work of Poetry: or, To Destroy Language

"If we could change our language, that's to say the way we think, we'd probably be able   to swing the revolution," says John Cage.

My own sentences on revolutionary poetics

1.   To restructure language is to restructure thought, to restructure possibilities.

2.   To scramble, if not permanently, which is impractical and will not lead to the   world we want, but temporarily, the world as we (think) we know it, the language   that binds us to the now, to put new ideas, new juxtapositions into play, new planets into orbit.

3.   As an instrument of "instruction" and propaganda, it is subject to the same pitfalls that all other forms of discourse and communication fall prey to.

4.   The avant garde is the "first wave," the ground work of consciousness, preparing the field.

Ecriture Feminine *and the* Petit Mort *of Writing*
One of my interlocutors was talking about dying little deaths, small deaths along the way of writing, this made me think of the petit mort, which is French for orgasm. And as I read Cixous and think about her ecstasy in writing, talking about the flesh at work in a labor of love, I think more and more about the petit mort as a form of women's writingxiii. This is all over Cixous. Her writing is full of ecstatic phrases about what it is to write. She does not fear the death of the author, either actual or metaphorical. Nor does writing, for Cixous, promise immortality. It is an in the moment activity. In "The Author in Truth," Cixous writes about "striking out for the unknown, to make our way in the dark. To see the world with the fingers: isn't this the act of writing *par excellence?xiv"* In her

manifesto "Coming to Writing," there are extended passages that are about losing yourself in mad love (amour fou, as Andre Breton wrote of), to writing, to a feminine writing. This is not a nihilistic death, as might be seen in Foucault or Barthes, but a joyous celebration of what it is to write. "The text, already the lover who savors the wait and the promise," she explains. "Text: not a detour, but the flesh at work in a labor of love"xv. As if she were taking the death of the author literally, then, she says "in the beginning, there can be only dying, the abyss, the first laugh.xvi"   In Cixous' definition of the text, I do not feel the need to repudiate stupid Derrida. I can accept that there is nothing outside of this text, this *ecriture feminine* in which all things live as long as they live. It is not a hedge against death   nor

a headlong dive into death.

It is not about immortality and "what survives."

Writing is its own joy,   its own reward   its own pleasure.

It is a petit mort that is meant to be shared.

It is a revolution in language that is meant to liberate.

It is a private moment, expressivist and confessional.

It   is   everything.

Bibliography

Barthes, Roland. "The Death of the Author," *Image, Music, Text.* Translated by Stephen Heath. New York: Hill and Wang Press, 1977. p. 142-148.

Barthes, Roland. "From Work to Text," *Image, Music, Text.* Translated by Stephen Heath. New York: Hill and Wang Press, 1977. p. 155-164.

Cage, John. *M: Writings '67-72.* Hanover, NJ: Wesleyan University Press.

Cameron, Deborah. *The Feminist Critique of Language.* New York: Routledge, 1998.

Cixous, Helene. *Coming to Writing and Other Essays.* Translated by Deborah Jensen. Cambridge: Harvard University Press, 1991.

Derrida, Jacques. "The Law of Genre," *Bulletin of the International Colloquim on Genre.* University of Strasborg, 4-8 July, 1979. Translated by Avital Ronnell. Speech.

Dworkin, Craig. To destroy language", *Textual Practice (18)2, 2004, 185-197.*

Lewitt, Sol."Sentences on Conceptualism," http://www.altx.com/vizarts// Referenced November 27, 2016.

Shuman, Amy. "Gender and Genre," *Feminist Theory and the Study of Folklore.* Susan Tower Hollis.

Endnotes for Laura Winton's <u>ECRITURE FEMININE AND WOMEN'S TRANSGRESSIVE WRITING</u> may be found in the Appendix.

ENRIQUE DE SANTIAGO
Chile

FRÁGILES TRÁNSITOS BAJO LAS ESPIRALES

Comencé a adentrarme en el mundo de la espiral, hace muchos años en la playa del Yeco. Deslumbrado por su geometría, aún no transitaba en las aguas de la surrealidad y en ese entonces aún no pensaba que en su estructura anacarada en realidad convivía la luz de las nuevas posibilidades de internarme en mundos supra-físicos de maravillosas posibilidades. Pienso hoy en día que aquello que vayamos descubriendo en el largo e interminable derrotero del Surrealismo, pasará a ser parte anexada de las realidades cotidianas, es quizás este el momento del viaje en busca de otro vellocino de oro, una ascensión al monte Olimpo en busca de las ambrosías que sacudan todos nuestros sentidos.

Nunca sospeché, que una figura curva desenrollándose en el tiempo-espacio revelara tantos misterios y me convidara a transitar como los antiguos primitivos, por aquellas sendas ocultas que se avecinan a nuestras realidades, sobre los vehículos de las formas de otros espíritus y las ánimas arcanas que abundan en las tierras del Canelo hacia el Sur. Tengo los navíos dispuestos a partir de hoy, para ver en cada pequeño detalle la más grande de las odiseas y hacer de cada uno de estas una aventura de insospechados descubrimientos hacia los confines de mundos de irrealidad, los que con certeza serán del conocimiento de este trashumante onírico.

Cada pequeño detalle en el universo es un portal al inframundo, un pasadizo al Xibalbá que se debate entre los múltiples planos dimensionales de una sinfonía de cuerdas cuánticas, cada beso es una arista para ascender, cada guijarro, la materia de la próxima gran explosión esperando desatarse en un mañana.

En el principio la luz estaba contenida, así como la materia toda y por lo mismo las estructuras geométricas que las soportarían, aguardaban las ecuaciones elementales y su momento para desplegarse en los infinitos planos y subplanos, pues siempre estuvieron ahí esperando dar una ratio que soportaran los mínimos y monumentales tránsitos, inclusive en nuestro devenir expandiéndonos como prediseñados cuerpos o a través de las invisibles designaciones.

Quiero detenerme en aquella figura geométrica que avanza, que determina los ordenes primordiales y los acota; La espiral logarítmica.

Es cierto que su asomo en el universo viene dada desde la primera mañana del tiempo, incluso puede que desde antes de la gran explosión esta nos esperara con su increíble diseño, el cual ya reconocían los griegos de la antigüedad. Pero fue Descartes quien la estudia en forma matemática incluyéndola en la denominación de curvas mecánicas, esto quiere decir, que su ecuación no es un polinomio, este hecho acontecido en el año 1638, fue comentado a Mersenne, quien también se interesó por esta forma de tan singular aspecto. Este comentó, que estaba buscando una curva creciente con una propiedad similar a la de la circunferencia, donde la tangente en cada punto corte la radio vector siempre en el mismo ángulo.

Ellos también descubrieron que esta misma condición es equivalente al hecho de que los ángulos alrededor del polo, son proporcionales al logaritmo del radio vector.

El nombre de esta curva eso sí, no vino de este estudio, sino que fue dado por el estudioso matemático Jacob Bernoulli que se empapó en profundidad de este maravilloso diseño de la naturaleza y lo estudió durante el resto de su vida, tanto así que mandó a grabar en su tumba la frase que designaba la propiedad de la espiral: "Eadem mutata resurgo" (Resurjo cambiada pero igual).

Una característica a la vista de esta espiral, es que la separación de las espiras aumenta al crecer el ángulo, esto significa que el radio vector aumenta en forma exponencial respecto del ángulo de giro, la espiral es distinta en radio desde cualquier punto de la espira hacia el centro de la misma, por esto recibe también el nombre de espiral geométrica.

Su ecuación es de la forma: r = Ce, donde r es el radio de posición, C una constante, k otra constante y theta el ángulo de giro, donde el ángulo es proporcional al logaritmo del radio. Una de las propiedades que nos maravillan de esta figura es que la espiral logarítmica es la única curva que verifica que su evoluta, su involuta, su cáustica y su podaria, que son a su vez una espiral logarítmica. Eso explica mayormente el "Eadem mutata resurgo" atribuida a esta espiral, ya que aunque me cambien, es decir si trazan mi evoluta, mi involuta, mi cáustica de refracción o de reflexión...siempre resurgiré semejante a mí misma.

Esta fascinante forma se prodiga de forma asombrosa en toda la naturaleza, ya sea en los objetos fractales, en los cuerpos ammonoideos del Cámbrico, Cretáceo o Jurásico (inclusive hasta hoy en día encontramos similitud de esta forma en los organismos Nautiloideos o en los caracoles). También se refleja en la proporción de crecimiento de numerosas semillas, sobre todo en los abetos, también en la manera en que determina la posición de las hojas en los tallos, la construcción de variadas galaxias, helechos, la multiplicación de insectos coloniales, o de los roedores y otras especies.

Es adentrándose en los aspectos cognoscitivos de la espiral como cuerpo físico presente en la naturaleza, es que surge la pregunta antes del desenvolvimiento corpóreo: ¿qué, la contiene y soporta como diseño estructural? ¿Cómo es posible que se mantenga prediseñada sin que se altere? y ¿qué la obliga a prodigarse de esa manera? ¿Cómo se anticipa este diseño como diseño primordial? es la cuestión razonable, y después el ¿Cómo y dónde la estructura se forma? Es en tiempos más que remotos, esto es claro, pero ¿En qué espacio y tiempo espera su momento para saltar a las formas de la vida desde adentro? pues no se conocen aproximaciones ni diseños tentativos como registro en los rastros fósiles. Pareciese que esta figura geométrica, fue diseñada por un plan maestro anterior pendiendo en la surrealidad del cosmos paralelo e invisible. Es el momento donde surgen las preguntas que plantean sobre los próximos y futuros diseños que esperan en ese estadio supra-cósmico, los que sin manifestarse aún aguardan para próximamente desplegarse en esta realidad conocida, o por el contrario en otras universalidades desconocidas para el hombre. Pues es en este campo cognoscitivo, donde el hombre surreal y metafísico es el llamado a emprender el viaje hacia estas nuevas e ignotas formalidades a través de la incorporación del espíritu holístico, en este despliegue holográfico llamado universo, donde la realidad termina por dar pistas de un mundo invisible dispuesto para que el hombre ávido lo convoque a sus sentidos, es ahí donde el surrealista se entromete en las verdades arcanas, aquellas solo dispuestas para aquel que a partir de los sueños, transmutará desactivando las trabas que el cuerpo físico nos impone para retenernos en la mal llamada conciencia, así la espiral pasa a ser uno de los tantos vehículos que llevan al ser que busca a los recónditos parajes del yo integrado al todo.

La espiral es la música para el que busca e indaga en pos de los mundos mas allá de lo conocido, es la barca que se ubica en la orilla de la realidad que invita a navegar trascendiendo las moradas de la verdad y las bellezas expandidas, pues es aquí donde ella ordena y se manifiesta y es también en sus construcciones invisibles que la sostienen donde ella se muestra al anverso de este mundo conocido, donde toda su forma provine desde cuando el mundo aún era joven. En ambos casos, ella se formó en los piélagos de lo desconocido augurando para los sentidos físicos el placer de la dominación armónica.

Quizás la explicación de todo esto, es que la espiral en si misma contiene una sucesión de rectángulos áureos, por lo cual esta misma es a la vez poseedora del número Fi, el número de oro, en el siguiente dibujo se puede apreciar que una y otra vez, se van construyendo cientos de rectángulos áureos tanto en sus formas reflexivas, como refractadas.

Sabemos que él número de oro se manifiesta en toda la naturaleza, tanto en organismos vivos así como en otras distintas formas constructivas o contenedoras, podemos nombrar como ejemplo, la disposición y orden proporcional de las falanges en todos los mamíferos, así como las estructuras proporcionadas de sus cuerpos, sujetas a un orden matemático llamada la sucesión numérica de Fibonnacci, quien descubrió este orden armónico presente en las emanaciones naturales.

Pero la tierra toda obedece a las influencias de la espiral. En la antigua región de Liguria (región de los antecesores de los Heracleos) surgen los monumentos megalíticos (dólmenes y menhires) estos puntos llamados "Puntos Lug" (en referencia al Dios Lug) (1) se distribuyen en la zona geográfica de la actual Francia de forma de una espiral logarítmica, ¿por qué? Se sabe que estas construcciones megalíticas interferían en la energía de la tierra a manera de lo que nosotros conocemos como la acupuntura del cuerpo (de hecho nuestro cuerpo está diseñado dentro de una gran espiral) hay casos en que estas intervenciones pétreas fueron removidas de su lugar, por ser objetos paganos (decretado por la iglesia en la Edad Media) produciendo trastornos como inundaciones de los cultivos con graves consecuencias, perdiendo así la tierra la propiedad adquirida por la ubicación anterior del dólmen o menhir. A todas luces se ve que además esta figura correspondía a una ruta de peregrinación pre-céltica, un camino ritual que tenía que ver con las correspondencias mágicas geodésicas   .

Es aquí donde yo coloco el tránsito omnipresente de esta espiral, con nuestro propio tránsito sin percatarnos de la disciplinada presencia de la primera en nuestra propia estructura corpórea, como así también lo hace en nuestro entorno. Esto de alguna manera da cuenta que el hecho de habernos estado ignorándonos en lo esencial, nos ha dado como consecuencia provocar desórdenes mayúsculos, ya que si las estructuras sostenedoras tienen proporciones exponenciales, los daños y sus consecuencias serán de efectos similares. Transitar o hacer él tránsito, en forma armónica en los distintos planos del entorno, lleva de una u otra manera al conocimiento cabal de los mismos.

El conquistador, el explorador que llega a nuestras costas desde el siglo XV en adelante y que desconoce estos ordenamientos primordiales, se convierte en agresor, un intruso en el plano, un agitador de exterminio, ya sea en ese momento o en nuestros días. Como dice Morris Berman: "La sabiduría hermética, como ha sido denominada, estaba en efecto dedicada a la noción de que el conocimiento verdadero ocurría únicamente vía la unión del sujeto y el objeto, es una identificación psíquico-emocional con imágenes en lugar de la examinación puramente intelectual de los conceptos." (2)

La vida es nuestro propio tránsito, separado, pero dentro de un tránsito global, masivo y complejo, hacerlo con conocimiento del reconocerse obligados a las estructuras fundamentales que lo ordenan, es reconocerse en este tránsito, como un propósito mas allá de perpetuar nuestro ADN a través del acto de la cópula, o ingerir todos los días calorías, esperando la oportunidad de volver a repetir esta acción en sucesivas oportunidades. La espiral nos habla de aquello que la sostiene mas allá de los planos físicos, pues sí hay algo que la sostiene en el universo tangible, llámese materia oscura, leyes gravitacionales o geométricas, a manera de planos sostenedores que permiten que se manifiesten.

Hay de todas maneras algo sin resolver, y lo dije antes ¿cómo se manifiesta exacta dentro de un espacio? y ¿qué, la obliga a no variar su forma desde fuera y que la mantiene desde dentro? y a estas formas anversas que presionan desde lo exterior, ¿qué las sostiene a ellas? ¿Qué las obliga o compromete con la forma logarítmica que cotejan? En fin, y más allá del cómo que preguntaba antes ¿Qué amarra o soporta a las formas que interactúan y a la vez soportan a la espiral? Y así sucesivamente en él o los planos infinitos y agregando además el cuestionamiento válido: ¿qué o quién diseña esta forma? pues si uno se interroga sobre la presión que ejerce el medio o entorno sobre las formas plásticas de los seres vivos, podríamos argumentar que en este ejemplo existen interrelaciones físicas (queda aún la duda de porqué el ADN, responde en forma de modificador en cualquier dirección en el cuerpo físico – es como si contuviera todos los patrones diseñadores) las respuestas quizás están tras los antiguos portales, los que ofrecen los secretos de la estructura del leviatán, aquellas amplias sendas de información que se manifiestan en este universo conocido a manera de diminutas grietas, donde quizás estemos hablando de otros universos con otra distinta composición formal o diseño, una distinta materia o inmateria, donde solo a través del espíritu liberado sea posible acceder, es decir, por intermedio de los sueños o tan solo a través del paso de la vida a la muerte. Sean estas las fases, quizás donde el espíritu (en los sueños) se prepara y aprende para el viaje definitivo y posterior (el trascendente) e incluso el primero de tantos.

Breton hablaba y describía al inconsciente y todo lo que ocurría en él o en sus manifestaciones, como un universo distante o un mundo desconectado. Si pensamos en aquello que soporta y obliga a las estructuras ordenadoras, llegamos a la posible conclusión de que hay puntos de sujeción entre estos distintos campos dimensionales, incluso algunos estarían carentes de tales dimensiones para así lograr un efectivo sostenimiento global de los cuerpos ordenadores (elipses, espirales, círculo, planos etc.) pero ¿sin dimensiones?

Es posible que la existencia de las dimensiones corresponde a los primeros actos o balbuceos en torno al verdadero y total idioma que rige las infinitas moradas multi-no-dimensionales, de ser así la distancia entre nuestro conocimiento de lo físico que nos aproxima tímidamente a lo metafísico, es de una inmensidad abrumadora, y somos en realidad pequeños seres limitados recién avecindados en un universo de formas y manifestaciones insospechadas. El absurdo, es la directriz inconsciente ordenadora, así como lo son los sueños y lo es también el punto de trascendencia espiritual dentro del orgasmo, cuando el individuo saborea brevemente la unidad en lo infinito, ya que este, a pesar de que se sostiene de una relación meramente física, tiene la capacidad de enlazar el armatoste carnal hacia estados superiores a partir de la no-conciencia. Esta también se contiene como capacidad trascendental dentro de la actitud de contemplación o desapego de la prisión individual. Hay también dimensiones adimensionales, y hoy conocemos tres dimensiones más una cuarta: el tiempo. Según la teoría de "Cuerdas" existirían otras 11 dimensiones. ¿Cómo son? Solo sabemos que existen por medio de las teorías de la Física y no lo sabremos mediante el uso de los sentidos físicos, por lo tanto no la viviremos, no la sentiremos, al menos que desdoblemos el ser para sentir de forma plena, tal vez la activación de la glándula pineal sea un manera de acercarnos a esos estados distintos del sentir. Sabemos que están ahí, al igual cómo sabíamos de los quasares por ecuaciones, hasta que fotografiamos su fenomenología lumínica.

Todas las espirales, desplegadas en todo el universo con esa inequívoca geometría con las precisas adiciones que en su avance de evolutas, son la base o sostén de la materialidad toda, permitiéndose coexistir armónica con los espacios a ocupar, las nuevas, de igual forma dan alojo al siguiente desarrollo exponencial. El nácar expandiéndose es como nuestra piel en el útero dispuesta a desplazarse en la evolución proporcional de sí mismo. Es el diseño invisible que se sostiene de las tensiones y distensiones de sus formas elementales, y cada tensión es transversalmente intervenida por una tensionante y otra distensionante, que a su vez, permiten que las masas criticas en suspensión espacio- temporal, soporten e impriman un impulso a los radio vectores originados desde el centro.

Estas estructuras que soportan al mundo, no pasan inadvertidas en este trabajo, a partir de estas ecuánimes razones sujetaré los protagonismos en áureas zonas, partiendo desde cualquier punto centro, y la composición no vendrá dada del clásico rectángulo áureo, sino que partirá proponiéndose desde cualquier punto de los planos y a partir de este y sus sucesivos crecimientos organizadores, así se dispondrán los elementos composicionales o de densidad critica en el objeto fenomenológico, el que seguirá su desarrollo virtual fuera del plano descrito y de alguna manera, intervendrá el espacio restante a manera de apéndice recordatorio en un breve espacio de los planos circundantes, esto estará obligado por la naturaleza de dicho cuerpo geométrico, que a la vez de potenciar la figura desde su centro único, debilita la forma para dar energía a otra circundante.

Tomando en cuenta el diseño del perímetro a usar, sería interesante ver dos o más formas provocándose en una extensión cercana e interferente, ya que parten de hipótesis distintas como una doble "arsis", cuya unidad formal plástica o tesis resolutiva estará dada fuera de los propios elementos plásticos. Es una suerte de instalación conceptual, des-instalándose para dar protagonismo con sus cargas opuestas de radio vectores desde la zona critica, lugar donde está el concepto, y hacia los centros en los rectángulos definitivamente plásticos, un Manierismo desconceptualizador (a la manera) no mi manera, sino la del peso organizador que contiene el exponer el objeto estético, no el social o el de las leyes severas de las artes. Se produce así, una poderosa relación por la simbiosis energética que se entrecruza a través de los radio vectores y sus evolutas, que a su vez se avecinan hacia las involutas opuestas fortaleciendo la estructura poética como tal, pero al mismo tiempo dando vigor al espacio virtual que ocupa el concepto. Este concepto ocupa un rol protagónico, pero a la vez clama por su descontextualización como concepto único dentro del todo, negando y afirmando a la vez su protagonismo, es como la segunda espira que se manifiesta espléndida y poderosa relegando a un plano basal a la primera, pero sin esta su existencia es vacía, por lo cual cualquier análisis decimonónico del concepto es un inútil tránsito si no se observa su entorno o paisaje, o mejor dicho su concepto vecino, su concepto de conjugación inmediata o futura. La siguiente espira depende del todo conceptual así como las otras sucesivas, así como el concepto depende del entorno universal para verse sentenciado como tal.

Los elementos dispuestos, sobre las espirales en el plano, aportan además elementos tensionantes anexos a los ya enumerados, estos dentro de su propia construcción y organización se reorganizan solo tomando como referencia el soporte de la tela o el poema, esta segunda lectura propone una suerte de anclaje para no comparecer sobre el concepto fuera del plano. Este peso de mayor potencia cromática o tonal, es el hilo conductor vía longitud de onda de diversa y dispersa índole, la que permite al espectador ligarse al plano en desmedro del concepto virtual, entonces el punto crítico plástico o tonal gravitará en mayor manera por la aspersión producida por los radio vectores de la figura geométrica, que domina el plano dentro y fuera de este y obliga al objeto en cuestión a obtener cierta dependencia y propone tensionantes propias que le sirvan de sostén y relación con la figura dominante sin perder su sustancia, su naturaleza también fragmentaria o su pertinente interferencia.

Mis manos las poseen, también todo mi cuerpo las contiene y este al transitar, se desplaza a través de ellas por los antiguos derroteros desde donde rigen al mundo.

Abajo el desinterés de las percepciones infructíferas de los legos o los necios, las mismas actitudes desde que los conquistadores transitaran sin descubrir las nuevas y antiguas espirales. A partir de ahí solo sombras sempiternas.

---

(1) Los gigantes y su origen, Louis Charpentier, Editorial Bruguera, Argentina, 1974.
(2) El reencantamiento del mundo, Morris Berman, Cuatro Vientos editorial, Chile, 1987.

PAUL McRANDLE
USA

THE GREAT MYSTERY

In *L'Art magique* André Breton locates a strange precursor in the gnostic belief that the image of a god can be infused with such strength and vitality as to terrify its creator. From the Romantics to his own day the "sentiment of being moved, when it is not one of being *played*, by forces exceeding our own will not cease to make itself sharper, more invasive in poetry and in art: 'It's wrong to say: I think. One should say: I am being thought' (Rimbaud). The entire field since then has been given over the question: 'What we create, is it ours?'" (1)

Magical art regenerates the magic that generated it. The through-line from gnostic theology to the surrealist image is a terrible autonomy. For automatist images like opium images are not evoked but come to the artist "spontaneously, despotically. They can't be dismissed, since the will no longer has force and no longer governs the faculties." (2)

The murmuring recorded by automatic writing need not be an externalized hallucination to lie beyond the writer's control any more than opium visions need be externalized. And the murmur may be both an infinite source of pleasures and of torments. Breton hallucinated large cats prowling through Paris traffic after prolonged sessions of automatic writing. But he goes much farther: "All of these [images] seem to testify that the mind is ripe for something other than the benign joys it grants itself in general. It is the only means that it has to turn to its advantage the ideal quantity of events with which it is charged. These images give the mind the measure of its ordinary dissipation and the disadvantages which that offers." (3)

A footnote citing Novalis' formula hones his point: "There are ideal series of events which run parallel with the real ones. They rarely coincide. Men and circumstances generally modify the ideal train of events, so that it seems imperfect, and its consequences are equally imperfect. Thus with the Reformation; instead of Protestantism came Lutheranism."

What is an Event? The Novalis quote appears again in *Logic of Sense* by Gilles Deleuze, whose interpretation teases out elements that occasionally parallel or contrast usefully with Breton's thinking. Deleuze argues that where Novalis speaks of two series of events—the ideal and the real—the distinction instead lies between the event, which is ideal by nature, and the accident, the event's actualization in a state of things. To clarify, Deleuze turns to Joë Bousquet. As Bousquet described in a *Minotaure* enquiry on the capital encounter of his life, in 1917 while in the trenches he'd shot and killed a German soldier thereby precipitating a battle in which his friend, a French sergeant, died of a terrible wound to the spine. A year later he was struck with an identical wound that left him a paraplegic. (4) During his years of association with the Surrealists, he came to an understanding of this horrific, doubled injury, seeing the events of his life as "in place" before he made them his own. He sought to make himself their equal in the sense that these events would only grasp the best, the perfect in him. In other words, he wished to be worthy of what occurred. "My wound existed before me, I was born to incarnate it." This is not the same as resigning oneself. "If to will the event is first of all to release its eternal truth, like fire from its fuel, it is to will to attain that point where war is led against war, the wound traced alive like the scar of all wounds, death willingly turned against all deaths." (5)

An Event is one with the mind sensing it—it is something new and singular that remains virtual, unknown until actualized by the mind. Events are in becoming; they are situations and their unique meaning combined. They aren't to be confused either with Plato's ideal forms or empirical experience.

For Deleuze, this means "willing not precisely what occurred, but something within what occurred, something to come conforming to what happened according to the laws of an obscure *humorous* conformity: the Event. (...) The brilliance, the splendor of the event is its meaning. The event is not what occurred (accident), it is the pure expressed within what occurred that signals to us and awaits us." (6)

Events string together singularities that are opposed to the ordinary; they are moments of tears and joy, sickness and health, hope and anguish, but also nodes, inflection points, changes of state. These singularities are pre-individual, non-personal, and a-conceptual, indifferent to the individual and the collective, the personal and the impersonal, or the particular and the general. (7) "I am being thought."

Novalis's quote appeared much earlier as an epigraph to Poe's "The Mystery of the Marie Roget," a story featuring his detective Dupin whose method (from "The Murders of the Rue Morgue") neatly sums up the Event: "it should not be so much asked 'what has occurred,' as 'what has occurred that has never occurred before.'" Dupin finds solutions by seeking out the peculiar in events, ignored or dismissed by the common sense attitudes of others, that lead him to the marvelous murderer of Rue Morgue (Poe, Surrealist in Adventure).

This is not far from Breton's conclusions in his essay "Introduction to the Discourse on the Paucity of Reality" in which he compares poetic witness with that of an explorer, and suggests the construction of surrealist objects that like an explorer's artifacts serve as evidence of their source, while simultaneously throwing into discredit utilitarian objects that always produce the same results. Our tired commonplaces and worn-out metaphors are traps: "The mediocrity of our universe, does it not depend upon our power of enunciation?" Whereas Breton finds in the hallucinatory power of certain images and the gift of evocation possessed by some a demonstration that we have yet to read the first pages of Genesis. (8)

Bringing novelty into the world, grasping Events, changes the world. "The image alone, insofar as it is sudden and unseen, gives me the measure of the liberation possible and this liberation is so total it frightens me. By the force of images over time *true* revolutions might well be accomplished. In certain images there is already the beginnings of an earthquake." (9)

So how to turn to advantage this ideal quantity of events we're charged with? Deleuze speaks of becoming the actor of events, playing a complex theme (or meaning) with more than a touch of *umour*. This theme only retains from the event its contours or splendor to counter the dumb sequence of the everyday.

For Breton it begins with dreaming and automatic writing, writing that cultivates its unconscious sources and speaks like a seer about the situations of our dreams. The two are inseparable, like the meaning and its event. Not only does automatic writing employ and transfer images from dreams, but Sarane Alexandrian points out that Breton's practice of recording dreams derived from automatic writing (10). This practice accustoms our memories to experiences other than the poor realities of our daytime lives, as Aragon noted in *Wave of Dreams*. Like Poe's Dupin, we must attend to the peculiar.

This isn't writing locked in the private world of the dreamer, far from it. Its complex theme, its meaning, is open to all who listen. It is the events of dreams rather than those of waking, the dream as continuously experienced in its peculiar organization night after night, by which we may find the path to the Great Mystery that will replace today's pseudo-mysteries (11). In part this is through openness to the dream, the murmur, and chance, and to those events in which these capture one another as if in a blinding flash that illuminates fresh paths.

Maybe like Bousquet we should speak of being worthy of our dreams, worthy of their absurdity, their singularity, their novelty, their unsettling nature, their infinite details, their continuity, their depths...worthy of our being *played*.

NOTES (translations are my own)
(1) André Breton, *Oeuvres Complètes* (OC), IV: 76
(2) Breton quoting Baudelaire's *Paradis artificiels* in *Manifeste*, OC I: 337
(3) OC I: 339-340
(4) Georges Sebbag, *Foucault Deleuze, Nouvelles Impressions du Surréalisme*, 277-278
(5) Gilles Deleuze, *Logique du Sens* (LS): 175
(6) LS: 175, my emphasis
(7) LS: 67
(8) OC II: 278
(9) "Le Maître de l'image," on Saint-Pol-Roux, OC I: 901
(10) Sarane Alexandrian, *Le Surréalisme et le rêve*, 147
(11) OC I: 319

PART TWO
RED RATS IN THEIR SULLEN CORNERS SPEAK

1 - JAKE BERRY
USA

Psalm: Transgression

I have come across the waves
to speak to you

The radio is wet with voices
They glimmer in your hand

You draw them into long violet chords
that unwind the storm
and summon angelic technologies

You drive the wind away
to scry the desert
for a language only sand can speak

What is your strategy to outwit death?
Will you play the Sepher Yitzirah like roulette?
Will you play the zodiac for a monstrous love?
What can you weave into time
to reveal its deceit?
Gravity is merely a trace of the grand disguise

When all machinery is obsolete
I will call you in those words made of sand
and you will hear light in a symphony
of astonishing colors

Your senses cannot contain them
They will overwhelm you
and pull you under

Nothing will remain but a child in the shade

Threshold

I have a basket of grapes for you

When I spill them
across the table

they spell a word
neither of us understands

Someday
when we are far apart
you will make its sound

and I will wake up
laughing

regarder la brume

lake of sot's gun he
ave yr fork out t hair tine's
fast sp lash il est tout mon
horizon)Pierre Bonoit(an
urinous moon sinks into yr
hand c'est la méthode gal
vanoplastique ma main te
touche les yeux PHONUL
GRAPHIQUES fog fills a
warehouse corpses wearing
just my shoes ;;;;;;;;;;;;;;;;;;;;;;;;;;;;;;;;
YOUR MOUTH BOAT wr
istless on a grassy field's yr
face breathes out breathes
out))))))))))))) s s   s
tumbles on a single step

...senda o nudo...

comolodo

floss the hamster sandwich tw
itching in yr mouth yr lentils
thicken eyes a sw allowed
moon behind the lenses
pools beneath a tree a
shallow forehead turns be
neath the hair was crowded
necks jostle from a shirt
tu bolsaboca de arena y ten
edores llena es lo que como
lo no comido ,restos del
principio del calendario cir
cular I sit and laundry sit and
lurch the stairs toward
air toward pit to war d
am munition in the dark

bare arm

gag it hot thin wind a
window ~ ~ ~ limb em
pathic cornflakes speak
your table's dim spills
lunch's last gleam the
wall stares back at
you tug and clench the
shot grin spins slow pas
t yr mouth the standing
cousin ,outer lint erect a
gate should ash decide
:oh pistol gloved beneath your skin

copa del tiempo

your slivered sky yr
retina churns and
coughs a mirrored ecel
ectric eye defolds a
baby thin as sticks
wind
still glue
behind yr jaw
ENDEFOCUSE SHADOWw
drawls across yr re
gazo fláccido ni tu
swivelled thigh will
rise ,offer the
pan masticado y líquido
con tu salivazo momificado
con tu salivavaso momificado

ay cómo tan sólo he nacido
- César Vallejo

issaid

pomade yr dribbly snore
retains to frame your stilling
burger lined with carpet
is your aftasleep what music!
ease of flood frontispiece a
book of nails and ghosted
hammers ,complex of a
postal drain behind your
sleep ,write an awful
is what throat retries wh
at th roat reretries or
wakes the same lung pillow
swelling on the windowsill
.walk out walk in walk past
walk spilled

bloody arm

3 - JOHN RATLIFF
USA

A Horse On A Handle of Wind

One can drive oneself mad in the moonlight
Watching kittens turn to tigers beneath the shadow of the blinds
Listening to rats in the walls, laughing, unseen parties beneath the bathtub
Being aware of faces peeking around the door frame, pulling   away when no longer in the peripheral;
Listening to door hinges crying out aghast in pain,
The house has old bones.
There are faces, sunken as ships, living in the closet between the coats
Sliding out to thud against the hardwood of my mind when I'm just shy of sleep.
Masses make their way from the edges of mirrors, along the walls, and across the floor,
Venomous monsters of psychomanteum, snake-like and smoky in their drift
As they slither to the door.
I must murmur a constant prayer to Helios,
Worrying the hem of these bed clothes to threads between thumb and forefinger.
Outside children are in the trees
Whispering with the wind
Plans for horrible murder once they've shed their leaves,
Conspiring with the horses
Who are suddenly at the fence line, pupils wide and rolling in their sockets
Showing off the white ghosts eyes mesmerizing and mad, saying:
"Come now. Go with us to whistle at the edge of the woods and see what comes."
Behind them, tomorrow's mist creeps across the pond of today,
Inch by inch bringing it to this side of the sunrise
One can drive oneself mad in the moonlight.

4 - LOIS ROMA-DEELEY
USA

Transport

I

In The Suppose, there is a forge
of hot coals,
and a hammer in the hand of an artist
who stands at his workbench
in the middle of a cave,
where fires
bellow against the wall of shadows.

The corners of this place
are filled with silver sweat
and spiders talk as they make their web;
they speak the language of The Suppose.

Shaking their heads from side to side inside their webs
every sound between this world
and the one made of silky dreams
will get eaten.

Here, dirt walls meet dirt floors.
and these right angles are a kind of proof,
(Don't you agree?)
an artist hands, hard at work,
(They always say this),
can make
all worlds come together.
(It must be true!)

See there? On the anvil,
an overlay of thinnest gold,
the idol–
shifts its shape
once a calf, now a woman—
it blushes
under the cyclops' eye
of a ball-peen hammer.
Within reach, but off to one side,

the artist's ham radio remains unplugged.
Spiders chatter
about how his childhood was mostly spent,
like so many uneaten plums,
in the service of the Queen.
(But she never found you, did she?)

and how those cold and majestic nights,
which he counted on as his last salvation,
fell down around his knees.
Only then he would sleep.
Because it took so many years

before he could clear his thoughts—
to believe in spider talk—
(You knew there were witnesses)
every other day became a work
not to spite them. Instinct,
the harvest moon, hangs over reason.

ii

Now the idol blinks.
Her beady, ruby eyes answers
the owner of the scent
above her own.
The artist has made his art.
Those blows, rhythm with heat,
must be bold. Just in case
there is the final escape, the last comfort of knowing

that one bead of sweat falling
from his parted lips onto the idol's face
could sizzle away
and become a black hole
where no one can enter.
(You are safe.)

But the idol's frightened to be that alone.
(and who will say it's your fault?)
The spiders' thinnest webs waver,
threads the artist's eye to his hand.

But, then, the jumping spiders attack beams of light:
impress this servant
of the Queen into observance!
(Is she the one who can't be controlled?)
Alarmed by tones too low to hear,
the spiders speak of a Royal presence.
There now!

He's done
the impossible, brought what was dead

into life and now,
unthinking, he sneezes twice
and the breath becomes a magic charm they dance on.
(You must be bold.)
But in The Suppose—
the universe snaps a picture:

Click:

iii

The Queen is very mean.
(so you say)

She rolls her r's on all four winds.
Quasars must pick them up,
exhausted from the ride.
Righteous anger
bounces about the sky–she has her needs!
Give me something to eat,
she says.

(it's your fault she's hungry)
Spider legs
crawl across an irate face,
itch the idol who would like to move away.
Curiosity chews at radio tubes.
Now, what could be the silence of The Suppose,
–from long, long ago–
is simple quiet.

iv

Another click:
switch:

The war brought him home.
Following the river running through his heart,

he finds arrowheads—
Apache tears–
scattered near
its steepest bank.
covered with dead leaves, the trail shook him:

Let them believe
in someone else for a while,

says The Suppose,
the child
of two mothers
could father one man.

That it might have been was destiny.
But the council room stood on a fault
which was, in fact, water weary earth.
There the Queen's subjects
gathered for his birth,
called a congress in the square.
The waiting ladies delivered
one shout to the unborn:
let go or die.
(Who would say this to a child?)

Tragedy took the whole nation.
His life began among ruins.

v

Iron rings hiss in the fire.
He's so surprised
when they spit
in the flames.
His story burns, word-by-word, tooth and nail.
Truth levitates from pain,

hovers–a lover's ghost—
who watches over all the wrong moves.

Static, more than once,
broke through
the cackling radio news
of yet another war.

Politely, he refused.

Now the spiders are his only friends
worth fighting for....
but a subpoena from the Queen
shouldn't be ignored.
Licentiously she grabs
whole landscapes
with one swoop of her hands,
stuffs blossoming orchard, a mountain
and several small meadowlands
into her mouth.
The great lake never fills her.
Consolation is a town of many worries.

Strange, that mangy bitch,
wearing a rhinestone collar,
breaks
from her trot.
She stops to sniff an open door.

Profit, the innkeeper and his wife
close up shop–
the Queen's orders.
(you, alone, you're alone)

As they hurry,
souvenirs spill on the floor,
cracking the given moment
like a brown egg.

Working. Working. Working.

The spiders form a union.
Some association of under classes.
Still it's not enough.

Strike
and the hammer sounds:
The idol looks from man to spider,
then back again–
there might be a riot.

Ruby tears mark her face.
The artisan,
who feels he has lived
too long any way he can,

finally gives in.

vi

The Queen
doesn't know what it means–
she's squeamish.
But particular

devotions force her to both knees.
Ten fingers intertwine
and clasp around the mine.
She inhales solar winds of gold dust thread.
But the spider is not the web.
Her servant
turns his deaf ear
against a dirt wall and stands watch.
Gray clouds break,

drenching the town called Consolation
with a thunder of empty threats.
The innkeeper hides in a bush near the hollow.
His Queen leans on her heels.
Being the soul of indiscretion,
he lights up a smoke;
she reaches for his throat.
Give me this!

Now her face gets as red
as the side door of a train
speeding through weeping guava grooves.
The web less spiders–

who say they eat *their* young–
(so it's true! you always knew.)

begin to work.

                    vii

The idol jumps from chair to chair:
an exchange
of a very basic nature
fills the air.
That quiet companion piece
to the Universe of *Suppose.*

In his thoughts,
(you, you, you)

the children
at the bus station seemed lost.
the artisan nods
to a pair of shoes pointed sharply at the wall.
He eases them into focus,
but couldn't bring these children home!

He could stamp their tickets
with a sign while humming radio tunes–

(how long is a long time?)
the war's almost won.
Their faces,
shapes of disbelief,
would feel so cool next to his cheek.
Crawling on hands and knees,
four inches–nose to ground–
he stops short before the idol.

Now no one knows
who or what it was
that breaks
the silence first...
but somewhere
in the far off wilds, a child

who was never meant to be
the subject
of her Majesty's
dying breath,
sails on a leaf...
rising higher than any thought possible,
the craft rides a stream of light–
spills over

your waiting hands.

5 - CASI CLINE
USA

DREAMS

I am standing in the living room of a childhood home, but I am an adult. I am naked with my back to the open front door, which makes me feel distinctly uneasy. However, I am completely involved in self-grooming. I look down at my breasts and they have lettuce sprouting out of them. I trim the lettuce with small garden sheers. I remove my left breast so I can more easily see the underside where the most lettuce is growing. I cut as close as I can to the surface of my skin, replace my left breast and move on to the other. Someone comes in through the door and interrupts me.

—

I have done some crime. As punishment I am forced to walk through a shallow, mucky pond while fully naked. I enter the pond up to mid-calf and I can feel slimy, slug-like creatures swimming around my legs, filling me with overwhelming revulsion. I am forced forward. I continue slowly into deeper and deeper water. I can feel the repugnant creatures slide across my skin up past my knees. As the water level rises, so does my panic. The water creeps up my thighs and the fleshy, swarming monsters hug me ever more eagerly.

—

I start as a human woman who gives birth, not in the usual way, but from the crown of my head. The resulting offal is a misshapen and lascivious beast with large sexual organs. My progeny tears off wildly in a lustful search. When some desirable being comes into view, it forces itself bodily into the victim's mouth and fills its insides with semen. This happens repeatedly while I look on helplessly. Out of necessity, I become a powerful god in something of the same form as my debauched offspring

70

but vast and ethereal, in which form I can then pursue it. When I find it, I fill it in turn with a sort of glowing and globular white light all the way to the brim. It is completely sated and dies, at which point I dissolve into the atmosphere.

—

I commit a murder in order to obtain a mystical power from my victim. I bury the evidence of my crime in the heavily wooded backyard of my second childhood home. As I brush away the leaves, I uncover layers of books instead of dirt. I become an elemental being of massive size walking across the earth in a few steps. I can see a pulsing sphere resembling an insect eye nestled in the mountains, and I go to it and copulate with it. The sphere is satan and all the earth's volcanoes erupt upon climax. I walk on and see another sphere, moist and tender like the white of an eye or an egg, protruding from the ocean. I copulate with it. The sphere is god, and all flowering plants bloom in an outpouring of fertility.

—

I am serial murderer, who seeks out elderly women for my victims. I take their lives with vintage sheers. Then I live in their house, wearing their dressing gowns, sitting at their dressing tables with their various bottles of perfumes, and performing their ablutions. As I reenact the little rituals of the elderly victim's lives, I can remember all their memories and experience their experiences. In this way I gain extra time for myself. I go to visit my grandmother unsure of my motives. In the end, I don't kill her, but not out of love as much as fear.

ANOTHER SEA

one step below the sea is another sea of insane ideas and haunting dreams and idle people staring into the void of time and space and forgotten nightmares. here the snow falls and freezes into sculptures of emotions and sensations. a sorcerer wanders through the sculptures and with maniacal magic makes them real and sets them upon unsuspecting swimmers where they writhe in the bloodstream until the time comes when they will crawl out of navels on spindly insect legs to reproduce.

a beetle is the perfect intersection of modern modality and asymptomatic electroencephalography. a beetle is not an ostrich you see? therefore they must bathe in the wine crushed beneath the feet of hermaphroditic youths. it is all so simple and so clear that surely now the world will be put back together again and the seas sink back into their places and the trees stand upright and the air come back into the lungs of the dead.

Disassembled heliotropes float aimlessly though the vast wilderness of hollow sky surrounding the end of the universe, now a single dark and infinitely dense pinprick in the numerical zero, making for a nice monument to futility and hunger or maybe even nematodes. naked mole rat deities visit this historical site on occasion, but always take it as a joke and leave with an unamused grimace. but the view is quite nice for the remains of consciousness peeking out of the tiny darkness and all the more lovely for its emptiness.

phosphorescent illuminations and pearlescent traceries delineate the passage of agonies and ideas and symphonies and fears in the aorta and gory chambers ticking away. a hidden map to be traced and interpreted by blood and bacterium. if only the wise paramecium may speak and tell the unenlightened what they learn on their cyclical journey to dust. then all may truly know what it is like for the world to end and then it may end.

a creamy pearl rolls down between full breasts into a navel waiting voraciously to suck it inside, deep down into the viscera of the undine there to sleep and dream. everything melts away, all flesh and water and rock until all that is left is the pearl as egg holding the offspring of all time, all thought, all ideas. every little epiphany and knot in the throat is contained inside it as it floats gently in the rolling amnion nursed by tardigrade and nourished by offal and effluvium, the pearl gently cracks...

A Shoebox Versus a Church Versus a Swimming Pool

Shadows dump the
voices of frustrated
pay phone calls into
the shoebox, with
an unimpeded boxcar
mustache that once
rode above lips tossed
with indigestion.

The church is filled
with hushed marching
and a brocaded cushion
feels boundless yearning
for the swinging
incense canister.

A swimming pool
can be baptismal,
so blue and rippling,
topped with shifting light
triangles, but it can
also be a fondue
bowl of greasy bodies
doing things that
humans do in what
some may call their
mortal weakness.

For the disgruntled
onlookers things are
at a maddening crawl
as they yell
for blue suede shoes
reflected in Cadillac
chrome, Germanic angels
lifted from Deutsche
Grammophon covers

aloft in trees,
roaring stadiums or
at least wrinkle free collars.

There is a slow
closeup on
a heavily veined hand
lifting a photo of
Uncle Divscek from
the still crisp shoebox,
its corners not yet
blunted or kicked around,
indicating there might
still be hope, that someone
has bought new sneakers
or wingtips for
a fresh school year
or job interview.

After surviving the
Battle of Bastogne
Uncle Divscek refused
to fly unless the
pop band The Beatles
were also on
the plane, reasoning
no God would take
them down while they
were so beloved.
Which is not saying much
for Buddy Holly or Patsy Cline.

In this photo
Uncle Divscek has his
parish priest by
the side of the
neighborhood pool.
A few days after
this photo was taken
two altar boys were
found floating dead
on the pool's surface
and Ringo Starr

was killed in a hunting
accident by the
Vice President of
The United States.

Tulum, 1989

The lean dogs with tight rough fur roam the beach at night.
Red Star Antares is so large and close you can hit it with a
tequila slingshot.

He self-medicates asthma with cough syrup, breathing wet
sandpaper as he hears the cry of the German sitting in the
outhouse as a snake lowers from a beam.

The beautiful little girl runs into their cabana, tells them to
come to her family's house.

The family's front room is warmly packed, the television
shows images of San Francisco wracked by an earthquake. A
young woman on the screen who looks like Bo Peep crouches in
a doorway convulsed by a belly laugh.

Silver Paranoia

Upon the shelf I am
my legs made of glass
first thing one morning
through me it shot
the March sun rising.
All my doors, windows
stolen from me.
One alphabet letter falls
counterfeit sentence
with the hard line

of clouds approaching.
Once I had it. Now
I have it, different
when I turn to you.
Just like this
plain as farm day and
Say I was by spooks
eaten; this is it
from the stash

in the glass I spent.

Examination

In palm
your final yellow band.

A corpse is one way to knowledge;
that sound against glass
color stopped, and spring's
meant for learning.

Death, the whitish

trace of movement is outlined
in an irregular spatter of feather.
You'll be in the green moons
of hosta, stilling the reflection.

Water. Wind. My back
against the hedges.

Volume

After a long time came the rain.
It was a passive affair, dressed in nowhere.
To lessen the need for witnesses
it came at night. Forget the pads
of cats. Its standing was considerably weakened.

You were near death so the whitetails
kept stepping forward, face stuffed with hosta.
The year's first hummingbird emerged
boring tunnels out of August and into
the shaken dice of a haphazard panic.

A family appears wanting. The antithesis
of ark begins to take shape in the park,
all twos making for fairy tale. Already the rain's
gone, drawn into the clean robin's clear song.
It can't turn up the volume up any louder.

8 – dan rapheal
USA

How Do I Hone Condensation to One Drop, Distill the Flow, Compounding Cake

A choice of clothing or furniture
From this perspective nothing's straight or continuous
We could drive there and swim back
It's not crowding that makes exit difficult but increased gravity
Refrigeration won't help; more flames means less for us
An alphabet of numbers; a jazz abacus
Without interest, taxation, commission, ID, brakes
Before i could get to town it went the other way
Night in a daylight basement
You cant scramble an egg without opening it
Back when awe-full was wonder-full
Behind the shelves are more shelves
The next valley north is an exact copy of this one;
if you go south you could meet your opposite

I couldn't live without glass
I'd let the wind in if it wiped its feet
How long can you hold up this world atlas
You can choose where to go or how to get there

Deign to disdain; indent with your teeth
I'd rather evoke than vote
Last night all the eggs escaped
We talk about transparency, but do we know it when we see it
He said give me some skin but i hesitated
These clouds all look like fenders
When a ladder becomes stilts
I'm smartest when immobile
Beyond ultra is what
Are fish in the ocean punctuation, the margin of error,
or what wouldn't dissolve

Hook Space

when the hook of space crawling inside me
opens like a premature freeway, sideways in strata of rain
we can trace the explosions of hyperactive seedlings,
patient geometric grasses etched with waves of birds
as regular as comets, relatives we visit once or twice a year
taking hour long drives across undeveloped suburbs
driving through the pores of this aging glass onion

making a flip book of my face by taking one frame each month for 30
years--
a voyeuristic legacy, my fingertips slightly concave from habitual beads,
as if some grace inside the words i repeat
energy penetrating from a molecular focus
to the outer reach of darkness, my good intentions
shaving fate, accumulating shields that filter out what i cant even
categorize,
names as costumes,   expectation,   narrowing with notches

as this jungled ridge is such a slow snake
guarding its eggs by swallowing them
if each hair on my head is the tail of brains menagerie
part of everything that comes inside never leaves
whether put to use or slipped through the fingers, circulatory press
gangs
drafting clumsily since they cant leave
no matter how fine the alleys get
the walls prevent puddling
except when rain without a sky
is the light from inside me or drawn there by the darkness

sky melts to a hat, as if the skull was clear-cut and flooded
as yeast tries another direction, leaving the gluten to its own devices,
letting sugar stay sweet til stirred brown by an insistent sun,
even glass needs to hold onto the memory of what pressured into it
like a bed sheet of the softest, safest lead
so we can evolve for other gravities
when the planet splits for personal reasons
as if it took the kite-string spider-webs from my neighborhoods
halloween porches
and laid them on top of each other to indicate urban structure,
overlapping without relating

Mind Mascot

Mind mascot, don't you drop your carcasses so soon. Let them percolate in the backdraft of bilge water. Heat is hot, bones are not, so bony carcasses are never warm enough, but at least they have splendor and much probation when they are betrayed.

Spoils The Night

Spoils the night like a huge wayfaring thing. Relaxes silently, the saturnine Saturday behind and beyond, but returning the day to its coffin of beauty. Your hint is there, a miasma of calm, a miasma of plastic sense, a miasma of uncertainty, and you likes it to death.

tideline

Moving with all this silence
I forget the weight of the tideline.
Behind me taunt the seagulls
as I follow God into the water.

I'm repeating prayers
from religion class,
the ones people swore
destroyed fear and brought on
miracles and triumph.

I struggle against two arms
speaking in one voice
dragging me back
to honor the drum
of living.

11 – JOHN OLSON
USA

The Emperor Of Macaroni

Speed is aromatic when it becomes lightning. Who are you? Ribbon is one solution. Moccasins are another. Density is magnificent with mermaids. Think of this as a phenomenology of reaching and reading and reaching for something to read. Of pianos and cockpits. Syncopation and garlic. Wax and honey, which are lieutenants of bric-a-brac, and dare to matter in a world of geeks and grossly inflated salaries. Even though, when you think about it, the sponge is every bit as brilliant as a whale, and a crisis such as this can loosen our frosting. I think it's wonderful that things exist. That the nose is naturally Zen and that one's chains are imaginary. Break them. Drop them. It's wonderful that magnesium can be a waitress and that the color gray can fall into the hands of a dwarf and televise the chlorophyll of a milkweed. That lips have their own brand of chivalry. That success can mean so many different things to so many different people. This hour will dissolve within the limits of another hour and various sensations will hatch out of that and become words in a sentence. Drop everything and run into the sky. Pasta is sensual because the streets are full of wasps, not because hope is cruel, and it takes courage to foster a load of despair. Hope is a delegation from a future that doesn't exist. Don't go there.

Official Anthem of the Ping Pong Litmus Association

Puff my unit. The crack I whisper. This zipper glaze honesty. Slither plunge configurational motion door. The crab lights up. This banana gurgles. This meditates my hirsute.

A thought flutters through a talk. I get behind a hint. It ushers a fuse to you. An ultramarine blaze.

We wear stepladder masks and crumple into frogs. A sloppy movement hefts a blue stigma. Necessitates it. We call the gnome. I scratch myself into henna.

The door gets its space over a batch of weather. My pasting for instance. The painter is innocent from swans. Smooth lake arguing increase. Opium is the pressed medication that opens diversion. If you have a spoon try the granite.

Burst dish. Atmospheric gargoyle chain. Acceptance romance. The hair has presence. The red bursts into robbery. Slouch world pulls its trickles to titbits. The snow steams on my glockenspiel.

Hold these brushes. A fiber dangles an academy. Initiates a Technicolor tomahawk. Hollywood here I come!

I collect myriad indicatives. We thicken enfoldments to marble it all.

I feel a certain wrench. A winch beneath the sun.

This will fill the scratch. The slow hold of pasting. The opened burst my impart. And then I subpoenaed a door. There rattled a crack. It burst its hinges and flew. There is a reason for radar. You know?

What gargantuan space brought meditation to hair?

The zipper puffed in heartwood and remembered the dishes.

12 – MAHINOUR TAWFIK
Egypt

The power of now

Like east and west is awake and conscious
The power of mind couldn't be less ominous
If the slave transcends taking over his master
Swirling back and forth from before to after

When all but now is a sense of illusion
Deriving its power from pleasure or pain
So fragile the mind is to abide the confusion
Of an identity derived from phantom of remains

Inattentive to the truth in this whirlwind
Handing over its limitless power
To the thought feasting upon one's mind
Cause its survival commands it to devour

For a moment I stepped from this battlefield
Not only aware of the events but conscious
Neither aiming an arrow nor holding shield
Not a convict not a victim but an anonymous

I've seen the master handing over the reign
Since then misery has dwelt the kingdom
Like the thoughts that took hold of the brain
Remorsing the past pleading future for freedom

Nocturne for Cabaret Voltaire

14 – JOHN J. TRAUSE
USA

What is Surrealism?

sparked an epidemic of juvenile obesity among the Albanian diaspora enthusiastic Vortigern with counterpoise as sanctioned by St. Collodion of Mayagüez Stalin-lipped, heh heh, get it in the house, babydoll.
They were uncertain when Zia Marta mentioned "junk in the trunk". Not good. I'll crush all your toy(s).
protesting the marwanification of new jersey, teasing treasure chest of dolly partonismus
deathbed lincoln diagonal   fragonard baise boucher
get me out of here.

15 – ANA PRUNDARU
Switzerland

Slumber

Nowadays, earth nests its lawless to dark soda foam beneath the sea. Sometimes, when sunless promises rain a splendor of inventory, distant grey waves that diaper and fence the lawless set them free. A perfectly symmetrical riot pushes out the sea's liquored shoulders. In angular splashes, they inch toward a blackened ceiling. And while hands rub, cut the world, an army of high-rise sentinels, with skeleton masks ruptures through soiled cotton towns, slip far away, stopping in front of a field of cacti. The sinful stop slippery, in the middle of the field. In the middle of the field are body bags. They lift the bags on their shoulders, to beach them flat at the foot of a rhinoceros-shaped stone. Hazardous corpses, locked in our names, are crushed to waste and shrubbery and shells. Later, the lawless must harvest suits out of the dispersing wishes we all once had. And while they do that, they grizzle to the snakes: are you listening? This earth wasn't for you. And the snakes say: Be quiet and keep working, you don't exist. And the sea sighs and wavers in invisible arms

Ireland

Stowaway

Lost in the planet wood, he imbibes solar ire
as he crosses the great divide.
A thought? An embryo?

He is dressed in caressing waves. The wind
is all salt, the infinity left ajar.
A silken lighthouse transmits his pulse
to the cloud womb.

Senselessness requires space. His face
is a non-face. He knows the way:
head first, then sideways.
He is the sum of his fears; the universe
the sum of its rubbish.
Capacity is an asset.

The slimy hemispheres are a ball of wait.
The museum of chance flowers with wily smiles,
one by one the portraits saying,
We had so many children
that some survived.

Neutral?

We fill our great big barn with little
sesame barns where we have emptiness
sorted and stored.

Barn guards burn candles of absurd
as their lips sip smog nectar.
They sin. They sing, *Eternity will suck you in, son,*
chew you up and then unsuck you.
We won't let anybody
empty our emptiness into theirs.

The earth's hair is parting the air.
We are a natal down, disempired islanders,
and we no longer cover our nakedness
with castles and coats of armour.
Green wigs on the green.
Keep safe and wear your horseshoes
and a farmhouse harness!

So are we finally half safe?
Are these pewter soldiers
neutral or neuter?
Surrounded by money, we surrender.
The survivors like to play a little flame game
with a blame brought in on the shoulders
of gap-fillers.

Distant fires, how they cool the skin.
World history, how it hisses.

Somebody Left a Feather on Our Credentials

This aluminium sky, dream-soaked,
as "vague and incomplete" as ever...
The world used to be a moister oyster than it is now,
don't you think? I mean, no one wanted
to borrow a name from the mind mercery –
who needed names? Or lacquered llamas?
In those times we meandered through the invisibility
of bats while our failed (flailed) flesh
contemplated levitation. Who was saying
he was left wing? We didn't believe in wings,
we believed in flying. The trick was
to make our anguish board a bird.
Temples were coming tumbling down;

mud huts (mad hats) had towering ambitions.
In the formula of life, all zeros were open mouths
waiting to be fed with grains of time.
Our away genes were dominant. Everyone
was sick of poets juggling galaxies
in their bedsits.
They eventually grew green tails
but that didn't help either.

17 – STEVEN CLINE
USA

Eliza

Eliza drags her nails across the back of the freshwater salamander. She returns a few months later and finds the illuminated country has been sacked.

"What is the next disintegration?", asks the orange malcontent. "Microscopic crabs flittering outside the body of the stillborn lover." she quietly responds.

The orange malcontent jumps for joy and waddles down the road. He comes to the decaying tar pit places himself in the center. As the tar sucks up his nostrils and he breaths his final breath he happily thinks to himself "No trouble for the piper, ma'am, no trouble at all."

Cenote

Night passes and I wake from an imageless slumber. I push myself out from my dark water cocoon and jerkily climb up the side of the Sacred Cenote, up towards the sun and its warmth. My worm-like body leaves behind a sticky sweet residue, and I sense each new step through the six slits of my face, these parallel cuts assigned to diverse range of sensory organs. She is near - her hide like leather and salmon, insides white and glowing. I pass the mouth of the cenote and slide into the forest. She lets out a low vibrating hum, letting me know she is ready. Triggered by this hum my body begins to secret a textured red honey from my facial slits. We touch under the decaying vegetation and begin to affix our massive prehensile bodies to each other. Her core bright and pulsating, spinning rapidly as our dark liquids seep into each other's heated flesh. Far beneath her third tail a small patch of hair waits, grows and retracts itself moment by moment. The circular flap near my stomach opens up and my euclidian organs ooze out onto the forest floor. Her hair stems grow bigger than ever before, wrapping themselves around my deposited innards and pressing them until they burst. From inside little tumble bugs scurry out and run for the treetops, trailing blackish smells. With my waining strength I pull myself into the folds of her shell and drop the rest of my deflated body onto her center. Poisoned fluids now dripping from us both eat our bodies and thoughts. We drift silently into death.

As the days pass our decomposing bodies will combine, one sweetly putrid flesh with no differentiation. At the center of this mound two eggs will form, nebulous siblings predetermined to repeat the cycle once more.

Metallurgy

Lilith called the community together and melodically sang out the newsflash. A metal egg had been found in the desert; it was hot to the touch and ribbed like a vertebrate. It was spherical rather than ovoid. The men jumped on their domesticated caterpillars and jabbed the pitiful creatures with a specially designed riding needle to get them to full gallop. The women melted into shadows and became red vocal sighs in the wind. They reached the clearing and saw the silver egg. It grew and shrank, breathing like an exhausted animal's abdomen after too much play. The men felt very aroused, and the women smiled secretively in the breeze above. The egg said "Whosoever can speak to me in a language undebased may have me." A man with a frog's face pulled a moist and well loved copy of Dante's works from his underwear. He read passage after passage from it, even including his absolute favorite verses, which he had underlined in dark blue ink and marked with a purple star, but was met with cold silence. Next the spectral women sang a little ditty about the movement of the stars and the menses of Jupiter's children, but were only received with a few skeptical "Hmms." Suddenly a little boy stepped forward, holding a pocket knife in one hand and an oyster shell in the other. He began to skin himself. First hesitantly, and then with more courage, he sliced layer after layer of pink from his fragile young body. Reaching the penis, he paused momentarily, spit saliva inside the urethral opening, and began the Great Work. Blood pooled around him, drowning entire civilizations of desert grub and sentient cauliflower in tidal waves of warm bodily juices. An IWW lumberjack's rusty bow saw, which had gone missing since the forgotten Portland wormhole strike of the early 1920s, suddenly space shifted underneath the boy's crotch, and he pressed down *hard* on it. He rubbed his perineum back and forth on it. He screamed on it. The red fluidic sweetness of his anatomy caused the metal egg to finally give birth to a majestic white horse with two X chromosomes. The horse called out to him in the coded language of extracellular fluids, a language only she and the boy could understand. Corpus cavernosum. Genital tubercle. Erogenous zone. A new ero-language untainted by capitalism had been invented. The bodies were not bodies and not spirit. They were neither but nowhere. A flea lodged inside the tissue of a leprosy snout.

"...and inside the vertebrae of the horse that old abused word "Liberty" finally shed its skin and became a new and freer vocalization, transformed into liquid, solid, and gas by naked homunculus translator...", as was later written down by the astute caterpillar and future leader of the zoological revolution, Leonor Asphyxiate.

An old horror film is played in triple forward motion, projected onto the back of the copulating human-horse insect by an autistic film buff, who's life's work is splicing together all sex acts committed on celluloid into the one grand Film to End All Films. These traitorous actors murmur that "...everything is erotic, that everything is sexual. That disease is the love of two alien kinds of creatures for each other." The scene cuts suddenly to film of a donkey humping an ape amidst swelling musical crescendo.

Mycobacterium leprae.

The men of the community collectively drop their pants and fondle their erections with both hands. Yes friends, this is what is often called by the crudely mannered as the "Circle Jerk". This mystical melding of fluids, this golden transmutation much maligned. The Sacred Circle of all occultists and optometrists combined. The women, still gaseous, sweep into the urinary meatus and expand the internals until those little male bodies go **POP**. Misguided androcentrism eternally dispelled in a massive sprouting of red tea and blue-veined flowers.

Meanwhile, the white horse and her boy are letting loose bags of brownish wet fur from the tips of their much enlarged and rapidly changing sexual organs. Undoubtedly the ORGANIFICATION of which I have often prophesied is on the cusp of its erootic rupturizing. A stream of rainbow tinted sperm shoots into the combined anus-vagina hybrid ingrowing on the left hip of the ecstatic boy who is rapidly transforming into a newly formed organism represented mathematically as:

$$\{[man/(girl + boy) - woman] \times (suitcase - insect)\}/0 = [(woman - woman) \times (-23)]/0 = [0 \times (-23)]/0 = 0/0 = \infty$$

For more ease in the telling, we will now simply refer to it as "Suitcase." Suitcase lets out a cry of painful joy, and bites down into the neck of the fluffy horse. It bites down very, very hard. The horse's head falls off and sprouts little spidery legs. It then scampers off into the desert to "find itself" and maybe enjoy a few erotic adventures of its own with some willing cactus or provocatively displayed lizard. Suitcase and Horse lay satiated and happy, giving each other mischievous and embarrassed looks. Suitcase wraps itself up in its sticky fluidic *kethoneth passim*, its spermatozoic coat of many colors, and says: "That was quite a fuck..."

"Oh, just wait till you see my old kink chest!" quips the massive bloody wound at the end of Horse's quivering nape.

But, to be completely honest, there was no longer any Horse or Suitcase existing at all. Merely an unending muscle tremor dwelling in the rocks and stones, bouncing around contentedly until that dimly perceived and mythologized epoch when cosmos swallows sparrow.

FIN

DE

M

Purr

Give me the bones of your lover. Give me the wheat made of clay.

Transform the night with the crackle of sunspots and sunrises. We will dig deep below - and devour the coughing stain of Antioch. Caress the mass of liquefied bodies out for their midnight entry. Struggle. Rub the decanter.

And why, you ask?

Because the tunnel must now be expanded, and the mountains must now begin to purr.

The Feminine Letter: Source of Ecstasy
(An Open Letter to Alphabets)

This story begins in the middle of a long night: I had been reading a tale in which the noted storyteller Baal Shem Tov appears and this was a dream I had in response to this reading.

A Jewish orphan born in Poland in 1698, Baal Shem Tov was a legendary personality of the heretical, Hassidim movement who sublimated in acts and words the aspirations of the mendicant and wandering Jews.

He lived in a period of particularly devastating pogroms. The remnants of the Polish Jewish community were overcome with sadness and despair. But Baal Shem Tov didn't feel the despair. His tales and parables were filled with joy. He was convinced that by changing himself or herself using dreams and poetry, a human being was certainly able to change the world.

One of his tales recounts how he found himself exiled, a prisoner on an unknown distant island, where for company he had just one other person. This individual seemed to be both a scribe and a disciple. But Baal Shem Tov no longer had anything to talk about or anything to teach. He was weighed down, defeated. He couldn't even remember his own name. His scribe-disciple was in the same condition. Everything had disappeared: all knowledge, every memory. And Baal Shem Tov pleaded with his companion (about whom he knew nothing) to tell him who they were and why they were there; but the companion broke out in a frightening laugh and insisted that he could remember only one thing. If Baal Shem Tov wanted him to, he could recite the alphabet like a young schoolboy. "We're saved!" cried Baal Shem Tov, "this is the happiest day of my life!" Painfully, the former scribe-disciple abandoned himself to the most profound despair. Half unconscious, he started to chant the beginning of the alphabet. Baal Shem Tov, in raptures, begged him to continue. Gradually, the two crazy men started playing with the alphabet and little by little they put together a new and extraordinary language: including whatever they considered remarkable and putting the rest aside. This is how they broke all chains and recreated the world according to their desires.

One night in a dream, like the storyteller, I found myself exiled on a deserted island, a total prisoner, without any memory. Unlike Baal Shem Tov, I was completely alone. The only thing I remembered was my female sexual organ. I vaguely recalled a few letters of a language that was not at all my mother tongue. My family knew only Ladino and Turkish–plus a little French and Italian. But I set about constructing an alphabet that, to me, seemed to resemble the Hebrew alphabet, the one I used to write my first texts as an adult.

But unlike Baal Shem Tov's ecstasy, an enormous anguish came over me. In this alphabet that I was reciting, I stumbled upon an absurd, shadowy, solitary letter. This was "ZAYIN" (ﬤ), a letter when pronounced in Hebrew or Arabic signifies the male sexual organ. (This is similar to English when pronouncing the letter c you refer to a large body of water.)

Suddenly I, too, experienced a marvellous ecstasy and I retained this ecstasy when I awoke. I had just dreamed that my sterile and sorrowful alphabet was missing one puny letter, but this letter was one I was able to invent.

Coming from a Muslim country and part of a Jewish minority, I was delighted by my impulsive revision of the Hebrew and Arabic alphabets.

In the mist, I traced this letter « ⱱ ⱳ » which had never signified anything. After this, everything followed directly. To this symbol I had drawn, I gave the name KOUS. This is an Arabic word which has been adopted by modern Hebrew. In both languages it means the female sexual organ and it is the object of ridicule as well as gross insults. Thus "motherfucker" comes from "KOUSSMEK." Nevertheless, KOUS and ZAYN curiously arouse a great deal of passion one for the other. In the mist, I began painting in black and white, but then a canvas appeared and was placed in front of me, colours next to me, and I found brushes in my hand. The "visible content" of these paintings is simple. In one of them, to the right of the letter KOUS there is a loving couple with a baby in the woman's arms. Beneath the letter KOUS is the letter LAMED (to study); to the right of LAMED is the letter SAMEH (joy). The visible content of the principal motif of this painting is simultaneously written and painted and they are easy to understand: "Study KOUS and experience ecstasy."

 For now, KOUS is unpronounceable. Where will we place it in our words? KOUS has no specific sound. But now it exists in an alphabet. It incorporates words of love, rebellious cries, poetic songs. KOUS is able to link them inextricably.

Where should we place KOUS in the literal world? Let chance determine where because I attributed to this letter the number 0, the infinity for the cabbala. In any case, it is always different from itself and moves around all the time like Baal Shem Tov when he recreates the world.

 Without eliminating ZAYIN to which it is linked, this new letter destroys the tyranny of ZAYIN's ghostly shadow. KOUS is able to undermine all languages. In every alphabet, even in an ideographic one, KOUS introduces the principles of gratuitousness and inexpressibility.

Possessed of all these powers, let this letter now make its way in the world. My dream can continue.

My Mother's Salon

Before the second world war my parents were quite rich, but the property of all the Jews in Istanbul, like that of the Greeks and Armenians, was confiscated in 1941. After the war, between my young childhood and puberty, my father rented a two-room apartment, with kitchen, in which five family members lived. The salon was as luxurious as an antique store, crowded with furniture and knickknacks (After her separation from my father, my mother was obliged to sell a number of these objects by financial necessity). My bed was hidden inside a lovely sofa in the dark hollow of this room. As a child I was often alone in the house. Having received my first toy (a doll) rather late, I was used to playing alone with the objects in the salon.

The games began with a ceremony: I walked around the big, round, solid oak table in the middle of the room. I nodded at the room. Then I took out all the objects into the enormous eight-doored buffet. I plunged a black African wooden spoon in the solid silver spice jars and the ceramic cups decorated with calligraphy. I imagined there were multi-coloured sweets in the spoon, and I distributed tea, coffee and chocolate services to the flat candlesticks, to the lacy bowls. Glassware from Beykos in my hand, I then offered other foods to the hems of canapés, to jars covered in turquoise opaline, decorated with flowers surrounded by gilt, to the gilded wooden armchair with the flowers surrounded by gilt, to the gilded wooden armchair with the violin-shaped back. The fabric of its yellow-silk brocade drank my magic soup.

Afterwards I sang lullabyes to blue earthenware cups from Kutahya, to flasks, to chairs with backs sculpted into the heads of lions and eagles, to the ivory Japanese woman who held an umbrella.

Then I gave first names (Ipek, Ayshé, Ali, Mehmed...) to the little dark-golden musical instruments, to the steer holding a trumpet surrounded by two nude children with eyes encrusted with brown shapes, to the bronze amazon laying next to a windmill, to the Chinese vases and the tulip timbales.

I started to have fun: I dressed up the pitchers, the shakers, the tiger surprising an antelope (in bronze with a green patina), the vermeil and "rat-tail" spoons, and I cleaned them.

I made all the objects talk to each other.

Then I made every movable object climb, swim, fly and ski.

I played Turkish popular music.

I placed the tiger, the amazon and the steer on the console above the mirror. I gave them other figurines for companions, notably a nude man in the marble (the only nude man I had ever seen in my life, with no name, and to whom I didn't speak), and I rolled coloured glass marbles between these immobile things.

I took a Chinese ivory fork, very long, and discovered my back by scratching myself. Then I scraped the divans, the insect-sculpted easy chairs, the greenery and the drapes.

I placed a crystal vase on an agate box. Above, I put a cup. Inside the cup, a lower pot, etc...I adored these superimpositions. I admired the balances thus created. I blew lightly on it.

At other times my games were more contemplative. I knew by heart the position of light and shadow in the salon, by season and hour.

Through a silver spoon, pierced by tiny holes, like a little sieve, which I made move, I looked at the rugs the tapestries and the image of two large chinese vases, taller than I. Seen through the moving sieve the images were fragmented. I got on top of the round table. The crystals of the candlestick, shaped like fat teardrops, and the part of the candlestick shaped like swans, brought me to the Water County. I made the pieces of crystal touch each other so I could see better. I didn't look at myself in the mirror, but regarded everything there was on the frame, between the golden leaves, especially the babies and the naked women.

From the windows, I saw the neighbourhood of Taksim. Sitting on one of the arms of the armchair, I imagined driving a bus and the people in the street took their places beside me.

COMMENTARY

To me it seems that in myself, the woken dream, spontaneous imagination and semi – controlled hallucination have developed rather than lessened with age. I continue to practice my childhood games almost constantly, and more intensely, but in a visual and interiorised manner.

I constantly transform the mineral and living worlds. I lend eyes and mouth to everything that exist. Imaginary relationships spontaneously establish themselves between everything that exist. When I was five or six adult disapproval could come at any moment, if they opened the door on my fabulous world. Today, however, my games have more replaced than left place for the "reasonable" world.

Therefore I live in a state of permanent hallucination which for many others would mean madness. This causes me only problems throughout my days. I simply combine these spontaneous hallucinations with an independent and creative life, with no relation to an alienated life or that of a child.

This development can be partially found in my drawings an water colours.

I play with mythic characters, objects which fascinate me, mammals, plants, birds, human bodies and everything which surround me, as if I were playing with the antique objects in my mother's old salon. Seeing as I was very careful not to damage or break my mother's objects, it is doubtless no accident that I have chosen a very fragile material, a translucent, even transparent, paper, for my water colours and drawings. The accumulation which characterised my mother's salon, and the anthropomorphism which I lent it, can also be found there. (In my canvases, each element is much more considered, and the plentiful world of my mother's salon appears less directly). That every creator uses his childhood world for his creation is well known. However, the challenge is to guard the magic of childhood also, to take control and go beyond the primary fascination of this childish world, oppressed and imposed in large part by one's peer group, to go search in another direction. The movement and interest of my work is to get rid all nostalgia, all obligatory attachment to the past, to fly and be captured, to be interpreted by myself again.

Paris, 1997

19 – SALVATORE DIFALCO
Canada

Defacement

Maybe some insomniac junk-sick man grieving his shattered life completed his masterpieces here. Maybe a sitting Pope reeling from absinthe commissioned it all in a funky dream-fugue. This is no Sistine, but almost, almost, why not? Small building for worship and venting: Gods, heroes, villains, some barely visible beneath the pentimenti of repentance and regret, the slimy patina of urban dissolution and human waste. Yet someone found fault with the whole operation, someone *owned* the space.

A homeless penniless loser showed his work the first time to passing vagabonds as a character-definition. "Don't judge me by my rags and bones, I am barely functioning, but look what I can do with a spray-can." No *Cadillac Moon,* but its neutrals, its violently upbraiding squiggles and luminous colour balloons obscure the visible struts and rusted pipes, the crusted filth, and spell out a lexical scream alongside cartoon-sequenced names crossed-out and followed by names crossed-out later.

In the light of day it is: mature work in a worldly communicative mode, at once a palette of crude simplicity—its visual rhyme very late *Riding Death* composed in a heroin wasteland with neo-primitive veering, its subversions unsubtle, its procedure violent. Last year he air-brushed a four-legged skeleton against the awesomely scumbled background, then a japan-coloured squid of absolute menace. This is the alphabet: alchemy, evil, heroin, black soap, rubble, shit and a corpus of crimes, serial crimes and petty ones. Freedom is nothing but freedom to fail, nothing to be gained from it, really.

"Do you think I purposely made what any person knows will change time and again? Everywhere, if all of us open doors and get out of the way of possibility— yeah, boom, ruptures. A car hit me playing street hockey, spent a month in hospital, broken arm, internal injuries, severed spleen. Pissing blood for a month. Puking bile. I was done. I was more than done. But moved by a small-screen *Gray's Anatomy*, I discovered the interior architecture of my body, and loved the way my body was component. Here is my arm, here is my leg. Here is my heart. And my skull overlooks the murder scene."

Later, they compared it to cave art, hieroglyphs, hobo poetry, cartooned Hitchcock films with a skinny bebop insurgency, a childish riot of scorn, an abandoned edifice spray-painted in an overcoat with big pockets, attacking high art in loose-jointed capitals— ALTERNATIVE LIFESTYLE—statements purporting a disaffected junky working spray-cans and footnotes, second-guessing his better self. Jonesing in the meantime. Hoping his dealer shows up before dawn. That's when real monsters come out.

Words jump at you like subway thugs, like terrorists alert to subversive possibilities, doubled with hidden meaning, sprayed as random nothings—crumbling cinder-block puzzles. The concrete teems with exquisite facsimile phrases and odd combinations of shapes first drawn on walls, cabinets and doors, before the house burned down.

Words turned, names blurred, turning to an inward language to dispel the ghosts lurking in the codes and symbols of the reigning superstructure, the one keeping him at bay, at odds, on the outs, full of doubts. Cross-out lines erase hurricanes of utterance, attesting to the mutability of language, the way words twist and turn according to status or mental state. People get caged inside them. People lose their freedom because of them.

"Everything I attacked I loved: or why would I have bothered? I despised it all only because I wanted so much to be part of it. I despised it because I knew I could never be part of it. I despised it because it silenced me. You keep asking what happened, what happened, what happened? For a more edifying or poetic account, sprinkle holy water over a man getting arrested and beaten into coma by three police officers after graffitiing an abandoned wall. Thirteen days later I died."

It has been said it was about *defacement*. Spoiling the appearance of something. Marring its beauty, or diminishing its value. Not masking its disintegration. Not beautifying the obscene. But someone was paying the electric bill. Someone *owned* it.

Three cartoonish cops took a moral stand one early morning: malevolence advances civilization, don't you know. Mr. Jones watched the nightsticks rise and waited for the blows to rain down on his faceless silhouette. Soaring above them was a twilit sky with nothing heroic or glamorous about it. Just the usual gleaming.

20 – JUAN CARLOS CASTRILLÓN
Mexico

Three Songs For Warriors

A TRILOGY OF POEMS

I

SONG OF AWAKENING

The heart is a spark of stubborn verdicts

The skull is an urn of expert contradictions

The rose is a quote of confused petals.

Blood is the reifying flow of history

The moon is the ecstatic pole of waiting

On the head of dawn mutes the stands

The clock is a mollusk riddled in the steppe.

The fog is the snail of holy war

Sunlight is the unrepentant dispenser of the cruel hope

Fire is the quickening molecular of our spirit

The butterfly is the accomplice of the virtual volatibilidad surprise in the genome

The guitar is the constant evolution of all plant species

The foam is the insatiable lip of waves

Rhythm is the ancestral demolisher of the untouchable

The voice of the woman is the biological agglutinator of matter

The web is the voracious cathedral of the cardinal points

Rage is the infinitesimal detonator of dendrites

Semen is the slime of cosmos inflamed in our mulish testicles

Saliva is the amniotic efflorescence in the salinity of the oceans

 Will accelerates the fate of stars

Let the enutation fill the conscience

 I'm not by depositing my mistake in her person

The light nourishes the nobility of the psyche

Let life grow to flood the sky

Let the morning deflower   definitely the tremendous tenacity of the darkness.

II

SONG OF SPOILMENT

 Air was the fetid dispossession of industry

 Water was a gradient detritus of trade

Land was a merchandasing excommunicated by usury

The whiteness of the snow

 was the myth of ancient religions

The melody of the cosmos was violated by the rumor of battles

Lungs were insects trampled by cancer

The liver was a floe melted in the sky

Rainbow Smoke maltreated the firmament

The extensive machinery oiled itself routinely with the blood of innocents

The kiss was a slogan of authentic misfits

Synapse was a busy

                    disagreement
                  with the night

The heartbeats were flashes of indigent purity

The flowers were dust discolored by the mire

Households were shelter for integer psychopaths

Clouds of flies
                  Harbored in the
                        coldness
                           our desire

The bread was rage of inaccessible hunger

The wine was conflict daily between tables

The apple was battering opinionated on the foliage

The ruin was routine

unblemished in the confines

Greed
        evaporated
                  conscientious
                      the genes of the race

Sleep records were looted obsessively

Chlorophyll was decapitated by destroyers experts

Tears were radioactive fragments of hope

Compassion between mammals seemed to become

an umbilical chain

against history
But
        amid the brutal waste
                  the spirit of the creators
                                    glare
                                    flashed
                                    budded unheard

until
        the universal transformation.

III

INTERSTELLAR SONG

Life will be the diamond fruit of work

Love will be the Flower Master of our conscience

We will harvest forests
        under the glare
        of the magnificent aurora

Fear will be a confusing figure
in awkward almanacs

Poetry will be the scandalous spike of destination

The planet will be a sacred drop in the Milky Way

The wind will sing foreverlife
        rhapsodies

The head will be the sphere of mutual understanding

Hands will forget
        the disorder of their fists

Resentment will be a vice of
        remote animals

Our eyes will be the necessary tool
        to recognize our equality

Selfishness will be a rudimentary
        dispossession of unfortunate beings

The thundering ocean perfume
        will inspire

secretions of the pituitary

The efforts of baked wheat
                    will satiate
                    the drive of the stars

Friendship among all species will promulgate

                    its equivalence
                    in all languages

The freshness of rain will wash off hygienicly the desolation of days

The laughter of the birds
                    will   pluck
                    exquisite
                    any kind of distress

The mountains
                    will trust
                    their wise encouragement
                    in the libido of youth

The mirrors' whispers will pacify
                    the probervial human jealousy

The magic will be science

                    of   generous teachers.

When at last

                    The cardiac momentum

                    in the structure of quarks

                    will organize

                    in equality

                    the roar

                    of bright

                    constellations.

At Mockerton

1) Undiagnosed

Done with remorseful tick and defiant tock - *applauding foreheads* - and wonted theorems behind tremoring hands on grey-areas and Neptune's one true pyramid, Mannequin was away, out The First and The Last, chasing his knees like two affrighted piglets.

Whilst stopped to pad for shag and countervailing that face (a maze of marbles above an uncharmed path and the path with no matter to acquiesce) and with no warning save the bluest sky, the crows of Birches House struck down, tossing his curls like spaghetti nera.

Officer Jenkins knelt, twirling a bloody feather between finger and thumb.

"Gone rogue," he muttered.

Ten days before Christmas, he'd found himself a salted mantle in a hospital bed as the radio bleated about how Mannequin had been arrested for waterboarding the priest after the priest sold him *that fucking useless car.*

No help, thought Jenkins, *no help at all.*

Officer Jenkins - perplexed - undiagnosed - knew he would never love again - and dragging a finger across the cat-tongued table top patinaed with vertebrae and brie, felt time, when marked by suffering, slowed terribly.

"Without amountfull provocation," he whispered, as the bartender tongued an eye socket with a commemorative tea towel. "An arbitrary mixing of genes, of generations - a meeting here, a smile there."

"A meeting, a smile," repeated the bartender.

"Gone rogue," said Daniel Jenkins, clicking his heels, clutching his side, curling up like birch.

2) Mannequin in The Cemetery at The Gate

In the shadow of sheaths, Mannequin wondered, sport-mourning at headstones toppled like a dyspeptic checkmate.

"Idiocy rarely outlives the idiot," he thought, picking at lichen. "Lena Duvil, Pymps Cansbloth, Johnny-Debbie-Tony - assholes one and all."

He knelt. Padding a blue tear.

"But it is these, who - committing no deeds worth commemorating and so compelling only poorly shopped grief - are kindest in death. So seat me with these assholes, these pricks and prutters and dolts and never the saints,

saints break hearts."

He stopped a moment to smooth his face, then continued on, toward the shimmering gate and his ship, pitched beneath the basilica's columns.

3) Mannequin Enjoins The Wet Words

The shuttle door rounded and rattled and Mannequin, booted in blue haar, appeared upon the ramp

"Behold, The Wet Words! . Debbie - *nose of father* and Tony - *hands of child* and Johnny - who would dare apportion credit for what laggers here today. No worries - you are here and not elsewhere and officially now and undisputedly now, *on the job*"

At precisely 12 o'clock NMT, as The Chrysalis puffed above the diamond barrels and petrified thirst separating each mastaba, Johnny - not Debbie - (certainly not Tony), finally addressed

Mannequin's snide mixing of endearments:

"You, *dear* Manaquin" he said, pinching his one eye, "can accommodate neither cardigan nor suit - your angles - which you vaunt without shame - are better attired to the vehicular snafu, *or worse*, The Vydronic Lift. "

"I could iron the oceans and parade them for hurricanes before you'd woken and wiped your arse," said Mannequin smooth as two-pack and slamming down the frame, spun The Chrysalis toward Mockerton.

4) Mannequin's New Car

Pymps Cansbloth - bound to a trundle in the embassy suite as Denholme ground his middle teeth and Lena Duvil's cemetery vase - *loved forever, forgotten never* - sloshed in the bathroom.

"....passsed the Urip belt, passsed arrows and mists and now unable to reach the corner shop for a bag of fucking milk...."

Cansbloth - landlord of Birches House - also vicar, undertaker, auctioneer, *car salesman*, gentleman to gentlemen - never quiet and always right - not the *the staff* - ALWAYS quite and never right - and who, pellucid as a Laomedeia morn, vantaged him for what he was - a bristlingly arrogant and (potentially) illiterate prick.

"I will require another," said Mannequin, emptying the vase over Cansbloth's toweled mew, "and if you blistered me again, I will enter and munch till sunshine."

Cansbloth - louder than a dawn delivery of swab, louder than full service - pumped the trundle til a fob dropped.

"Marvelous." hissed Manaquin and picking it up, sliced the binds with his twitchy finger and left for lunch at The First and The Last.

5) A Brief Tour of Birches House

Birches house - Once rendered plump and summered by the crisp and crispy loch set, was now a decrepit fella - sagged and boneful and grey

But Despite this, *or perhaps because of it*, the lobby thrummed and every vacancy was filled. In room 24, Lena Duvil, estwhile fashion retailer and now, since Manaquin's intervention, well along her grand tour. In 47, 9 and 12, the Wet Words respectively.

The crows (wronged as scrolls troweled and brushed and cooled beneath glass for children, bored and bruised, and retirees smelling of small denominations) - always took the attic, always arrived late: always waited till buckets were tucked in dark city cupboards and the arcades deluge had slowed to a drip.

Mannequin, of course, always roomed at The First and The Last.

6) Grey Area 6

Lunch at The First and The Last and the sun was fierce through the fly-sucked side lights as Mannequin ordered Another And Another untill his mind settled upon dreams of time travel and riches.

A drip of McMurphy's Swab hared his lips as he reclined in the box window watching the river babble at salmon as if it was their driver and they were its fare.

His food finally fell and as he sat flicking up slips of white bait and brie, he wondered why, since they had no need, human babies cried so and why, rather then open at both ends, human units didn't simply unfold like boxes.

"Why," he shouted, as if kicked awake.

"Why?"

"Yes why," said Mannequin, pushing his plate away.

He composed himself. Turned.

"And this place - why so high?"

"So high?"

"Quite a climb, to this pub," he continued, wiping his mouth.

"To this pub?"

I've heard of a grey area, Grey Area 5, along the westerly road, toward Ballyhate. Is this place also a grey area?"

"A grey area?"

"Never mind, just do me one simple courtesy."

"Courtesy?"

"Bring me a fucking drink."

7) An Interview (Mannequin not present)

Once his colleagues had left for home, for sneaky swab and stewy biscuits, Jenkins locked the foyer door and crept into Interview Room 1.

He knew the words - spoke them as if HE was Mannequin.

"Tell me the first thing.."

"The *first*?"

He crossed his legs like he was knotting refuse.

"Cleanliness."

Images, not words - a torrent of sounds and smells - the rumbling bass and brumes of rib chop; the evening's brick-shots of laughter and invitations despite his accusations.

And later the shiver, the skulking sense of mortality as he spent nights researching trees to screen his property from theirs: silver birch - 2 meters in 20 years; white pine - 4 feet in 8 years...

"Godliness" - nothing cleaner than a cliché.

"Do you always answer with clichés?"

He sought another - a joke in lieu of an actual honest answer. But clichés were sometimes difficult.

"Beats me," he said.

8) Abducted

Four klicks from Mockerton (on the road to Ballyhate) they found their grey area within a triangle of ruined drystack and tearing Jenkins from his bed, lowered him onto a wheelchair at the center of its icey parlor.

Jenkins opened his eyes, saw Debbie kneeling at his side.

"Your tomorrows," she said, "as abundant as carbon wash. Swimming with X, fishing with Y and no loss, no grief, no untethered storm or wave that reaches high as you drift through soft harbour lights"

"Yes," whispered Jenkins, feeling her hand at his cheek.

"And every decision a harvest.. "

"Imagine," said Jenkins smiling as Johnny tapped and yanked, totalling each smile.

"Look now - the sun is close, gravity is folly...."

"Of course."

"And six kingdoms of guilt because you want to but *can't* blame yourself?"

"Silly..."

"Daniel!"

Over green-sheaths, an ambuscade of clouds, crows arcing like shot.

Too late - Tony grabbed Jenkins and swung him high.

Then away, disappeared into dots and lowered on the wings of crows, Jenkins woke sideways, subsumed in fluids too copious to all be his own.

9) *Diagnosed*

Jenkins wakes and sees a pageant of disease - Wet Words, lanterns between bee's tongue and sweetclover and slowly (robed in butyl) Manaquinn: foreheading: fresh milk, episode three; *a swift trim* and laughing, (embarrassed for embarrassment) and propelled by no concessions save last year's breeze, Jenkins lifts swollen fists and commissionaired by a single tear

is *gone.*

22 – LAURA WINTON
USA

Glossolalic Angel Dada

Angels with harps   cherubs   speaking
Arabic writing Japanese in strange tongues
Divine chords glosso   lalia
Angels with axes   while   Dadaists
Break code break chords break ranks break . . .
In the war Nazis sing (of)(in)the spring   le *printemps*
Cherubim   play divine chords while codes
Break in the hands of Angels   turn
To dust as they climb the forbidden walls
Carve stairs into stones   from
Stones   into stairs   into codes   into stars
And Dadaists play electric   Romanianresistance
          Germans   carved from stone   miracles   wrought
with axes,   Angels and Germans speak in Arabic
          Chip away like a sculpture
                         Strange like Germans who speak in tongues
               like
Lengua like language like songs like guitars   rock   and
resistance   like axes and harps and   Tzara breaks
Images like a sculptor shows faces   for
Who they are and show   Nazis   and break
Guitars like code   it takes an angel of Romania
To be dada,   glosso lalic and sacred and
Break Nazi guitar codes and play chords on harps and
Have wings with which to fly.

121

Bus Reverie

Watch the woman whose face has frozen that way--a pouty frown that makes demands, takes notes. The old women watch everything with great interest, like a child's first car ride; their heads bob forward and side to side as if trying to see above a crowd, watching a parade. I lean my head against the window leaving neighbors and familiar streets incognito, forget myself and all my words forget they ever happened, write them in a lost language only God still reads.

And the moon . . .

You should have forgotten I lived once on the moon, rooted for the stars among asteroid ball diamonds, pitched meteors at the earth, queued off in dodgeball teams and freeze tag. The fingertips of children turn to Midas, casting plaster out of play; do you remember the ancestor pets? spirits of the hamsters, scattered gerbil ashes and dog crosses, their bones sanctify your altar. Just before the sunrise you can hear everything. In the absence of day's light a black hole will draw you a new galaxy, new suns will shine and burn

themselves out again like cheap light bulbs. Once upon a time you believed everything was a fairy tale, taught by the trolls the secrets under the bridge, fell into sleep so deep you never needed to wake, chose your apples wisely. The Hierophant, God's yes-man stutters through our death sentence, a syntactical stay of execution. A tickle in the throat is Scheherazade's new story, holding tomorrow in suspense.

23 – ERIC WILSON
USA

Hole

"You are now old enough to bathe on your own," his mother said.

"But the water is deeper than before," the boy, not yet six, replied.

"Your head will be above the water line," his mother replied. "You will be fine. I must cook the bird for your father. He might be coming home tonight."

"But the water will get cold," the boy said.

The mother said, "Not for a long time. It is almost boiling hot. Please get in."

The boy persisted. "But what if the lights go out?"

"They will not," his mother urged. "Now get in. You are dirty, and your father might be returning."

The boy's mother left the room. The boy became naked and stepped into the tub and lowered himself into the water.

The water in the porcelain tub looked white. The whiteness turned the room around it black. The boy sat in the darkness the white made. He loved the warm water on his skin. His mother was right; the water would not get cold. He leaned his head back against the rim of the old tub. He fell asleep.

He awoke choking. He had slid under the water. He heaved himself upward and coughed and spit until he caught his breath. The water was now cold, and it was no longer white. The darkness in the room did not make the white whiter. The dark was dark.

The boy cried out, "Mommy, mommy."

His mother did not come.

"Mommy, mommy," again young the boy cried.

Silence.

The boy would have to climb out of the tub on his own.

He placed his hands on either side of the tub and pulled his knees to his chest. But before he could rise from the water, a hole opened in the ceiling and through it rushed hot white light and a blur of gray and the water splashed into his eyes and it stung them and then he forced them open and hovering above him was the man from his father's book, giant and silvery in the glare, circle of black for a mouth, no eyes, nose, ears, in his left hand holding by the hair the head of a boy, in his right an ax so black that the light turned it white.

The boy could not cry Mommy. He could scream. He screamed a scream.

The man dropped the head into the water. The water splashed into the boy's eyes. He closed them and opened them. The man was now holding the boy's hair with his left hand and was raising the ax with his right.

A wall of smoke slid between the boy and the man from the book. The smoke was hot. It burned young the boy's eyes. Someone was lifting him from the water. He was carried out of room into the house. He was outside the house. He was in the yard. It was cool. His mother was holding him, chest-to-chest; his chin resting on her left shoulder, like when he was a baby. He was turned away from the house. It was almost night. He was still naked.

"Mommy," he said, "the gray man from the book dad made came through the ceiling."

"No, child, he didn't," she replied.

"He did," the boy said, "and he had an ax and he was going to cut my head off, just like in the book."

"No, boy," his mother replied, "what you saw was smoke. The bird I was cooking for your father was burning in the oven. I had gone to the woods to pick blackberries and forgot the time and remembered it only when I heard you scream."

"I screamed when I saw the gray man," the boy said.

"Son, you did not see the gray man," his mother replied. "You saw smoke. You screamed. You saved us. The house would've burned. I threw water on the bird."

The boy did not say anything. He closed his eyes and did not want his mother to put him down.

She whispered in his ear, "What's happened here is grace. That's a stroke of luck saves you from dying."

She put him down. He did not like it.

"I guess your father isn't coming," she said. "Let's go clean up the mess."

Then the boy's father was home. It was later. His father had made a new book. It was about a boy who has a ball the size of a man's head, and the ball is magic. It turns everything it touches, except the boy, into water. One day the boy is very thirsty, so he touches the ball to a book, and the book turns to water, and he drinks the water. When his parents discover this—they did not know about the ball, which a gray man had given to the boy during the night—they scold him. They tell him never to turn anything to water again. But the boy is thirsty. In secret, he turns a plate into water, and then a jug, and then a chair, and a table. When his parents find out, they scream at him. The boy is startled by the scream. He drops the ball. It bounces toward his parents. It touches them. They turn to water. The boy is sad, but he drinks them anyway.

The father read the boy this book soon after he returned. At the end of the book, the boy. —he was now almost nine— asked his father, "Whatever happened to this boy?"

His father replied, "The boy walked all around the world, turning everything into water. He was extremely thirsty. Eventually he turned the entire world into water. But he had not thought that there would be no place to stand. He drowned in all of the water he had not drunk. Nothing was left but a world of water and a ball the size of a man's head floating on the water."

"That is a sad story," the boy said.

"Perhaps," his father replied, "but also true, for it tells us what kind of people we are. I brought you a present."

The boy's father reached inside his coat. He was always wearing a coat now, a thick gray one. He was always cold. Out of his coat, he produced a purple ball, the size of an apple. It bounces, his father said, and he dropped it onto the floor and it bounced back up and he caught it.

Soon after that the father left again and did not return. The boy played with the purple ball. He loved to play with the purple ball. He dropped it onto the ground and it bounced back up and he caught it.

But one morning the boy woke up and the ball was gone. He always placed the ball beside his pillow before going to sleep. But the ball was now not beside his pillow. Nor was it under his bed, or anywhere else in his room. Nor was it in the house he lived in with his mother, the house whose kitchen had blackened walls. He could not find the ball outside, either, not in his yard, not at the edge of the forest.

Where had the purple ball gone?

The boy lay down in his bed. He was sure that last night his ball had been right beside where his head now was. He did not believe in the gray man, as he once did, so he did not wonder if the gray man had taken his ball. Then he thought that he might be in a dream, that all he had to do was wake up from this dream, and the ball would be right there, beside his head. He reasoned that if he closed his eyes and fell asleep in this dream, if this was a dream, then the dream he would have in this sleep would not be a dream, but reality, himself as he really was, waking up and finding his purple ball beside him.

The boy closed his eyes. They had not been closed long before he heard crying the kitchen. It was his mother. She cried in the mornings.

The boy opened his eyes. He looked where his ball should have been. It was not there, but he did notice for the first time a small hole at the base of the wall between his room and the bathroom. The hole was roughly round, and just big enough for his purple ball to fit through.

He sprang from his bed to the wall. He lay on his stomach and looked into the hole. He expected to see the bathroom on the other side. He hoped that his ball would be there.

But the boy saw darkness in the hole. He should have seen light, light from the bathroom, through whose window the morning sun shone. But he saw darkness.

What was this hole?

He wanted to reach into the hole to find out if his ball was there, but he was afraid. Anything could be in this hole. A rat, or a spider, or something else—even though he no longer believed in the gray man.

The boy wanted his purple ball very much, though. It was the last present his father had given him, and he liked dropping it on the ground and watching it bounce back up and then catching it.

The boy was afraid, but he overcame his fear. He reached into the hole with his left hand. At first, he only went as far as his wrist. He felt nothing but cool air on his hand. Then he pushed in farther, up to his elbow. Still nothing but cool air.

He was growing unafraid. There was nothing dangerous in this hole. He reached in all the way to his shoulder. That's when he felt something round. But in touching this round thing, surely his ball, he pushed it away, out of his reach. He stretched his arm as far as he could, but it remained out of his reach.

He thought, I can use a broomstick to pull this round thing, my ball probably, toward me. Then I can reach it.

The boy removed his arm and ran into the kitchen. His mother had stopped crying, but her face was still red and puffy.

"I need a broom," the boy said. "Where is a broom?"

"In the closet," his mother replied. "Why do you need a broom?"

He thought it best not to tell his mother the truth. "To sweep my room," he said.

"What?" his mother said. "What's gotten in to you? You've never swept your room before."

"I'm going to clean my room to cheer you up," the boy said. "I'm going to clean the entire house."

"You are a sweet boy," his mother said. "That is very nice of you."

The boy took the broom from the closet. He hurried back into his room.

He lay on his belly again and extended the broom handle into hole. He felt it touch something. This had to be the ball. He then positioned the handle to the left of the thing and slowly tried to angle it back towards him.

But the thing rolled away to the right. It had lost contact with the broom handle. The boy slid the handle to the right as far as he could, but the handle touched nothing. He slid the handle to the left as far as he could. Nothing. He slid the handle back and forth, once, twice, three times. Still nothing.

Where had the ball gone?

"What are you doing?"

Had someone spoken?

"Son, what are you doing?"

It was his mother. He turned toward her voice. She was standing in the doorway. He pulled the broom from the hole and stood up.

He still thought it best not to tell her the truth.

"I was sweeping," he said, "and just noticed this hole and wondered how deep it goes."

"How did that hole get there?" his mother asked. "I've never noticed it before. Did you do it while you were playing?"

"No," the boy said.

"Don't lie to me," his mother replied. "I hear you playing roughly in here all the time. I bet you did it while playing with that ball your father gave you."

"No, I didn't," the boy said. "I swear I didn't."

"All you do is play with that ball," his mother said. "I'm sick of it. Give me the ball."

"I don't know where it is," the boy said.

"You lost it?" his mother asked.

"I woke up this morning and it was gone," the boy replied.

"Are you lying again?" his mother asked.

"No. I swear." Now the boy would tell the truth. "It rolled into this hole."

"Impossible," his mother said. "You've disappointed me again."

She started to cry. She walked out of the room.

The boy's mother did not speak to him the rest of the day.

Preggo

Oh Preggo. Preggo Preggo Preggo. Poor shame. The Preggo sits in the old dark wood. In holy hood.

Accompanied by despondent lakes; the dream deferred. Rather than doze off life, she awakes. Her hermit eyes, greet her sunrise. The sun shines; lets it be known the path to where she's lived. The shimmer is cast, winds the road leading to. Winds the vines grown old, entwined over her home. Holding her estranged and into place. In the mad ghetto forest, where she stays. Put.

This welt-hut, shanti shack of smut. Obscures aforementioned nature. There is too, an opening to a place called home. Going nowhere, but she does go there. Where the love and lack there of, roam. The kettle, the stove - they've all gone to phobia of use. What a house she might blow, if misused. There is too, dry porridge. The flimsy carpet. Oh Preggo. Mold adorns the carpeting!. Getting around, would be walking on eggshells. And so that happens.

As a matter of factor. Most peculiar, is what capacitates her most beloved closet. Eggs, eggs a plenty. White shells unscathed, never cracked, but always made. What lies inside, neither lace nor you can tell. Yet.

Sorry for herself, no. She is a secret. She tells herself that. Never parting ways with secrets for anyone cause of boredom. By golly, don't get it wrong though - she's pretty sweet for a heart. She's gotten away with her face alone. This smooth feature - the angel exterior. The Preggo voice is made of solace and lace. Make sense of it while you can. Her love is big, if you can get to it. And her love of dinosaurs was gargantuan.. Its quite the embarrassment. Secrecy will do her some good. Only does this day come, that she decides to leave where she's from. And so that happened.

She made peace with what she could. Growing out of holy hood. All she holds, are her eggs and her wits. Perhaps to be scrambled along, but she'll take the risk. Outside by the wagons, she placed these orbs in, Till at once, she was all done. Thats it, all her eggs in her baskets. Setting out on her playdate. The Preggo departed ways.

Strayed from stars, she walked. Led by her friends gosh and darn, she walked. Pondering all the plunder, rape, and pillage, she passed. She sat, to notice the leaking, when a few of the eggs cracked. Oh Preggo. So sloppy. Such the floozie, and not the sweetie sweetie sweet heart you set out to be. And making amends, she cleansed and she cleaned. Mustered her strength, cussing and continuing.

Okay, running. Elegance had come to come undone. More of a mess came reporting for duty. No clean up. No reason to. No reason to slow down. Go through the shoo flies, she thinks. No more delay for whatever may come her way, Exnay on the pleasantry. She tugs these peculiar wagons. Frittering under twigs, batting away the ones fallen nil. Beaten them all left and right, by leaps and bounds!. The Preggo will be the strongest to ever survive life!. However, this is no place where the bed bugs bite. There is too, an absence. With elegance on the leave - don't know how her luck will hold up. Non-survival is eminent.

Dead light, green light. No safety will arrive. No eating a diet of small potatoes could prepare her. And so this happens : the bog comes on, the vision goes looking. Her hermit eyes await signs of a pathway, from away this gas. And through the foul, after dancing her feet several steps, a high wall makes itself apparent. Stone towers reach high, and become apparent. So does the draw bridge and the large door she's drawn to. Incredibly, badly.

By now, all the eggs have cracked but the one. Down she glanced. The eggs eggs cracked, out came the yolk yolk yolk. The lone survivor, was carried away to the unlocked door. Ditched her trollies she did, as she went inside.

As vast as empty. Harkening back to the life she left. No longer a surprise that surprises. The time was took to explore rooms, adjoining rooms and all the first floor. Till the stairs stopped her. Winds the stairs, grown old. Go, did she go. Up high, down low. Too slow. Oh Preggo.

Too far. She came this way, egg and all, to this last room. But she was not greeted. Why she couldn't have. Not with the conditions of whom she found. Dozing off life. Imprinted upon his throne, with his book of law opened. There, sat the king. Chillin' like a villain.

Sleeping like a sheep. Made of shambles, bones, and meat. Here is serious business in all its seriousness, fast sleep. He had already hit the hay. He had hit the hay hard. The open book, gave Preggo the smart ass idea to leave a gift placed between the pages. The Preggo doubled back, mistaking her footing, for grace. The king awaked.

A joke isn't being told. Someone is dying in their sleep. That, is now no longer the case. The silence gets clogged. The Preggo is back in the real world. Where the forgiven and forgotten, run the risk of running into her. And boy did his holyness ever do. The dear old dad, she never had, knew. The opportune moment came and went, and came again, he knew. He was going to be a father again. Daddy was reunited, with daddy's little fuck tart. The incest princess.

And so this happened. The Preggo lived happily, ever with her father, after finding him. Only, it didn't happen - and so this did : the comfort of the room ceased its illusion to trust. The towers in his voice toppled, against her, backing the bitch into a ball. Scares her shit, *this little tiff. This little tiff, on this little hussy. Language, colored itself a potty brown. He spoke, breathing this slow smoke. Polluting all the airs, and heiress.*

The Preggo did not respond. Eventually the last egg would have to, on her behalf. She contributed enough neurons to this relationship. So be it happiness apart from each other, that kept them apart so long. Her heart knew what his would bring. Nothing. His holiness is next to bitchassness. His holy shit, she'll no longer take. She couldn't possibly. This will sew him up with so much. As always. As it would seem, being mad at him forever, saved her the trip of getting in the mood to, this next time. As oppose to when last he estranged her, for her egg defect.

Enough of this. No more charity compliments, bating, or gifts. The last gift had slipped. There, in his lap, sat in his crippled literature. There, the book slid between his legs, cracking her egg. Wide open. Down they looked. Where the contents irrigated her breath. And so this happened.

For it was in this one, this special one, that a meteor appeared. One special, warm and rocky meteor, that signaled the end of this dispute. And this great sound arose from the sky, till it became audible to the Preggo and the king potty brown mouther, dad. Outside, meteors were beginning to fall. They came one by one, till they came all. A reunion was taking place. Overtaking the castle. Meteors, meteors a plenty. Greyish-black and weighing crazy. The family came down, to see the birth of its baby. To kill destroy its captors, gone on the hating spree.

The king rat, squealed like a pig. The meteors digged. Pecked the castle. Chewed it to ruins. No remnants will be found. Rubble ash and rubble. Finds the ground, and settles down. These space rocks, smash the king. These rocks rip through nicely. They break the body, they leave their mercy back at the galaxy. The blood meets the egg for the first time. The Preggo noticed. She smiled. She did, and she took it in, cause she knew. Another meteor arrived. She smiled wide. The meteor paved. Killed her breath. Totals her skull. Smashing the smile out of her face. Hello, hello muerto. Hasta la vice versa, worldwide. The meteor family spread and rejoined, till all that was left to do, was rejoice.

A man died today. A girl died today. Oh Preggo. Last one out, is a rotten egg. And so that happened. The meteors came to pick up their child. They broke their kidnappers legs. They broke their arms, ribs, and heads. And that is how you came into the world, dear reader. My little meteor.

And your love of dinosaurs, was gargantuan.

. FIN .

25 – KIARA BREEDLOVE
USA

Bambi

He kill her. A little bit every day. Drag her out to the big oak tree in the middle of the overgrown backyard and do the deed.

A knife dug just deep enough to draw the red rivers from her veins. He wants her pain, every slow sip of it. Once she give up, he done. The nectar ain't quite as sweet without the struggle.

She lies there, the dirt and dead leaves crunching into her split open veins. Then she spot me.

I don't look away. Hiding ain't my thing. I stare at her like she there for my entertainment. And she is. Why else would she let him drag her all way out to the yard?

I suppose she expect me to do something. Yell at him to stop. Let her alone. Guess she think since we both bleed by nature, I'm supposed to cry over her spilled blood.

It's always hunting season for her kind. The doe-eyed and helpless. When the rifles is loaded, I ain't never jumped in front of no Bambi. Not about to start.

She still there. All big-eyed and wounded.

"You always watching. Why don't you do something?" She lob the question at me like I'm the one beating her upside the head every night.

She look surprised that I ain't all ate up with guilt over her wretched situation.

I light the cigarette I been saving all week, take my time feeding it to the flame. Take that first long pull, then let the smoke curl out my lungs like I'm made of fire.

"Why don't you?" I ask.

Bambi ain't got no answer to that.

She turn and limp back into the house, mad as hell at three people, two of which don't care.

I go back to my herbs. Back to minding my side of the fence. No thoughts of Bambi and her doe-eyed problems.

...

It's late when he start all that hollering again, home from the Hyundai factory and hungry. The roast burnt. Mashed potatoes ain't got enough butter in 'em. The tea ain't sweet or cold. But his blood sure is.

I sit on my back porch, waiting for my own supper to finish cooking, and listen to him throw Bambi from one end of that clapboard shack to the other. She screaming for help that won't come. Begging for mercy that ain't there.

After while, he must sling her into something too hard 'cause she shut up. Then he start hollering, the frantic kind now like he give a damn.

The day's dying outside. Something doe-eyed and helpless might be joining it. The fireflies is lighting up the yard, dancing with the night as it eat up my garden.

He stop hollering. Start giving out they address, telling someone to please hurry. His poor deer done hurt herself real bad this time.

It get kind of quiet for a few minutes after he hang up with help. Then he come out the back door. Breathing all heavy, sweating and looking 'round like a runaway slave.

He catch sight of me and my eyes.

Though we done been neighbors almost a year, he look at me like he ain't never seen me. Which may be true. Men like him don't never see women like me. And when they do, the gaze ain't nothing nice.

The cat who lend me her company sometime come creeping up the alley behind the houses, squeeze her way beneath the fence, cross my yard like her name on the deed. She see him, look, but don't stop, eye him like she don't too much care what he over there doing with blood on his shirt and a bag of broken dishes, long as he don't mess with her. She make her way up the porch steps, slinking her midnight body across my bare feet. Me and my sometime pet go inside for supper, leave him to find his own conscience.

Sirens tear into the middle of nowhere quiet of my little street. I turn on some Nina Simone, listen to her tell a man to either love her or leave her. My chicken with the french name is about ready. I pour myself a glass of the wine I drowned the bird in, sit down in front of the player, put my feet up on the coffee table.

The cat come in, have herself a seat on my lap. I stroke her dark fur, happy to have something living and breathing in the house. I know she belong to somebody. Ain't no street cat this clean. But I guess she know I need her more than her owner. Or maybe she like me 'cause I buy the fancy cat food.

Supper start to smell like it's done. And it's right on time. Nina's voice working on me, touching something I don't want touched.

I open a can of food for my guest, set her dish on the table next to mine, because she won't eat no other way. Like a proper companion, she wait until I arrange my chicken and summer vegetables on a plate, sit down and say grace.

We only started eating, when a bunch of none of my business start knocking on my front door. I tell Nina to sing a little louder.

The knocking stop. Me and the cat keep eating. Nina keep singing, determined to root out something I need to stay buried.

I'm still smack in the middle of minding my own, when someone else's business start knocking again. It's at my back door this time, knuckles rapping on the frame. Ain't no ignoring it when it come up all dressed in blue, looking through my screen door, measuring the slice of my life it can see.

I tell the cat to stay off my plate. She look at me, no intention of minding. I walk slow over to the record player, ask Nina to take a break. I make my face smile, not too much, just enough. A smiling woman living alone make folks wonder. Especially, a woman like me, who done did what I did. And this man in blue been looking at me sideways since we was both in diapers.

I stand at the screen door, but don't open it. He can hear me just fine from out there.

"Good evening, Ms. Vincent."

"Officer," I say, staring death into his eyes.

"I'm sorry to bother you. But it's about your neighbors, the Fishers, over here on the left." He say it like a question, like he ain't sure I got neighbors. Far as I'm concerned, I don't. "There's been a ... an incident."

An incident. So that's what the police call it when a man use his fists to sing his wife to sleep. I'm not surprised. I was *an incident* once or twice.

He stop talking, waiting for me to pick up the other end of that rope and tug on it with a question of my own.

"Did you maybe hear anything? See something?"

More rope I ain't picking up. I lift my shoulders up and down, acting as simple as he think I am.

He take off his hat, and tuck it underneath his arm. Then he hitch up his belt. His pants don't fit him right. I'd offer to take them in for him. But his sagging waist and crooked cuff is more of the same none of my damn business he trying to leave on my doorstep.

"Ms. Vincent, please." His officer tone take a dip. "She's hurt pretty bad. The EMTs are taking her to the hospital. Her head's split clean open."

For a moment, I wonder what Bambi's head must look like "split clean open." Was it all red and raw like a piece of beef. Did it squish out the crack in her skull, gooey and sticky like silly putty. Plain curiosity was biting at me. But that wasn't my side of the fence territory.

"I didn't hear, or see nothing, officer."

"You sure about that, ma'am?"

I nod.

Things get quiet. That eerie kind, where you start to notice things you ain't never realized was making so much noise. Little things, like the tick tock of a clock.

I don't keep no real clocks, don't even set the digital ones on the microwave and stove. Time don't make no difference to me. No sense keeping up with its passing, when it don't care none about mine.

I look at his wrist. It's his watch making the noise.

He got a right to time. It's always on his side, like everything else. Bambi, even with her doe-eyed problems, she got time too. And she got this man in blue caring about whether her old man had something to do with her head splitting clean open.

I got a wayward cat, and a drunk chicken that's getting cold.

The cat come up beside me, settling herself at my feet. She glance his way, ready to make him scarce if I say he ain't welcome, which he ain't. I pick her up, ignoring the bit of my supper she got stuck in her whiskers, because she making my life seem a little less threadbare in front of him.

"All right, then. Well ..." He let that part hang in the air a moment, still dangling something for me to get caught up in. "If you think of anything, please let me know."

I nod again.

He put on his hat, tip the brim to me. I laugh at that, a quiet one just for myself. Not too long ago, this man in blue sat across the table from a defense lawyer and denied ever knowing me. Now he acting all polite like I ain't who I am, and he ain't who he is.

"Goodnight, Ms. Vincent."

"Night, officer."

The cat and me turn and go back to the table. Just as I'm setting her down, the screen door creak. When I look around, the officer is in my kitchen. Everything in me get real still and wait.

He take a step forward, his polished shoes tapping the cracked tile. He take his hat off again, hold it in front of him. His eyes go all soft, like a clear sky. I ain't never liked when a man look at me that way. Too hard to tell what's coming next.

He take another step, too close now. I move back, put some safety between me and him. But he reach over and take my hand, the one that don't work too good. He set down his hat and run his finger over the scar stretching down my wrist like an ugly mountain range.

"That night. Nick was ..." He look up at me. "I never forgave myself for what he did to you."

I look down at the scar. There's another one like it on the other wrist, just not as deep. Each year, they get even uglier, never fade. Neither do the memory.

We had the officer over to our place. Nicholas worked an early shift that day. So he and his crisp uniform that I pressed the night before, walked through the door at four in the afternoon, instead of eleven that night. I helped him change into his jeans and the new sweater I bought that matched his brown eyes.

When the officer rang the bell, I answered the door and led him into the study. I fixed them both a drink, went back to the kitchen where I belonged, let them talk about things I was too something or other to understand.

Supper was on the table at six sharp. All the silverware was in line. None of Nicholas' food was touching. His peach tea had four perfect ice cubes and a lemon wedge on the glass rim.

I was doing everything right. But then, the universe noticed I hadn't messed up yet.

The officer made a joke. Nicholas didn't think it was funny. Probably because it was about him. Before I could catch it, I laughed.

I started stuttering. Nicholas started hollering. Then the officer started stuttering and hollering. After that, came the silence.

I knew what to expect from Nicholas. He was a man who thought the world owed him something, and by default, I did too. I was willing to pay my debt. Didn't want or need nobody getting in the way of him taking his due.

But the officer, he was supposed to be different. His momma and daddy had said so. He was one of the *good* ones.

That night, he showed me there was another kind of man in this world. There was ones like my Nicholas. And the good ones like the officer, who make it alright for them to do what they do.

It's good he ain't never forgave himself. I ain't forgave him neither.

I slip my hand from his.

"Mona Lisa." He say my name like it's a new car he got his eye on. Like it's already his. And all he got to do is sign on the dotted line.

His radio start to crackle. Another officer call him back into the fold. He turn it down, still eyeing me.

When we was six, I caught him looking at me the same way. He told his momma he was gonna marry me that day. She found him something to do that didn't leave no time to play with the help's daughter.

Took me another ten years to understand the reason his momma always told me he couldn't come play. He was one of the good ones. The good ones didn't play hide and seek with the maid's kid. The good ones didn't marry little girls that wore knockoff Keds, and only had two second-hand dresses to her name.

The good ones smile, and leave little hand-me-down girls to pick the dirt out her own skinned up knees. But they get altogether crazy over a doe-eyed Bambi.

Another boy in blue come up my back steps, walk through the door, pay no mind that this a home. His hand already on his gun. He take one look at me, and undo the holster.

"Everything all right in here, Officer Miller?" He talking to his partner, but still staring at me like I'm some rabid dog he ready to put down.

"It's fine, Collier. I'm just asking Ms. Vincent some questions."

"You sure?" He take another step over to us. "You know she's the one who—."

"Rick." The good one turn to the other one, drag his hand over his face. "I got this. Why don't you go across the street and ask Mr. and Mrs. Bullard, if they know what happened over there. If anybody saw something, it was one of them."

Officer Collier keep looking at me. I dare him to do something with that gun. The good one step in front of me, blocking my stare. His hand reach back, pull me close up behind him.

"Collier. Please." He point him to the door.

It take him a minute, but he button up that gun again and get out my house. He leave the screen door swinging open, giving whatever flying nuisance a way in. The good one go pull it up, and lock the wood door. Then he face me again.

"I know, you heard what went on in that house tonight." He rest one hand on his belt, the other on the back door. "You know better than anybody what happened to that poor girl."

The good ones and their Bambis.

Wonder how many kitchens he stood in asking, if they knew what happened to the chief of police's wife. If they'd ever seen Chief Nicholas Calvin come out the back door of his cute victorian house with a bloody shirt and a guilty bag of dishes. Was I ever doe-eyed and helpless to him?

"I told you, officer. I ain't see nothing. I ain't hear nothing."

"Derrick." He shift his weight to his other foot. "Call me Derrick ... please."

The cat come rub her head against my hand. She been waiting for her cue. Guess she figure if things ain't gonna get juicy, we should go back to our evening.

"I think you should leave now, *officer*."

The cat jump off the dining table, and make her way to the sofa in the other room. I ask Nina to grace us with her presence again, turn the player up enough for her voice to fill the house.

His mouth say something. But don't nobody here care enough to listen. Nina got her own problems. The cat don't give a damn, 'less it's something in it for her. And me, I reckon the words ain't meant for me no way. He leave my world the same way he came, shutting the screen door behind him.

...

Next morning, one of the ladies who knew me when I was Mrs. Chief Nicholas Calvin come by. She stand at the chainlink gate to my garden, her hands tucked real close to her like she afraid some rock bottom might jump on her skin and follow her home.

Never liked her much. She always made sure to point out a bruise I didn't cover well enough, or ask how come I could sew the "most darling," little dresses and short sets, but ain't have no kids of my own.

The whole town knew why I ain't never have no little one hanging off my hip. Even if they didn't know, they could guess. And it wasn't because the Lord hadn't seen fit to bless me with the gift of life. It was because He *had* seen fit to bless me with a man like Nicholas—a blessing who never took off his disguise.

"Mona, I need your help."

No hello. Just start talking about what's going on with her. She a Bambi, too. Not as pitiful as the one next door with her split open head, but still.

She going on about "being in a bad way," and how she ain't got nobody else, and she hate to ask.

I know why she here. What she like to do when her husband at work. She want that bad way that gone come out looking nothing like her husband, and a whole lot like the man just passing through from wherever, to go in the opposite direction.

Her husband one of the good ones, like the officer. Honest enough, but too damn afraid of they own shadow to stand for nothing. I know he know what she do. He know that oldest boy of theirs, the one named after him, ain't no more his kin than I am. But she must know this "bad way," is too far off mark to pass.

She wait outside, while I gather up what she need. I ought to give her the wrong thing. Then next time I see her ducking and dodging me at the grocery store, I can ask her how come she skin and grin in Jesus' face every Sunday morning, but two of her children don't look nothing like they daddy.

But my momma didn't teach me about herbs, so I could be evil. I take it out to her. Explain everything real slow and careful.

"How will I know, if it's um ... successful?" She look around like anybody here give a damn what we talking about.

"When you not holding something that's screaming for your breast." She turn her nose up at me.

I could tell her what to look for to make certain the product of her afternoon petting ain't still multiplying and dividing itself into proof of how wholesome she really ain't. But nobody ever told me. You see enough of something, you learn how to tell when it's beginning and ending.

She try to pass me something over the fence. I tuck my hands in the pockets of my jeans. I never take nothing for cutting off "bad ways."

Even if I wanted a thank you, she don't offer one. We just nod. She tiptoe her way along the side of my house back to the cab she got waiting. I go back to my garden, and try to convince myself I just did some unknown clump of cells a favor.

...

They don't keep Bambi at the hospital but two days.

I watch him help her inside from my kitchen window. She got a bandage on her hand. Few cuts and bruises on her face. They must have put her head back together, because ain't nothing oozing out nowhere. She a little unsteady on her feet. But don't look too bad. That boy who do yard work for the Bullards will still jog across the street, all shirtless and full of teenage hormones, when she offer him a glass of lemonade.

Bambi will live. I go back to my coffee.

A little while later, someone come knocking on my door. I ignore it. The knock come again, louder this time.

I answer it, ready to tell whoever that whatever they need, I ain't got. There's a man on the other side. One that I was expecting sooner or later. Seeing as he seen my eyes the other night, I figure there's something he want to discuss.

"Afternoon. How you doin'?" His voice sound softer up close than it do when he screaming at Bambi. It don't fit him. He too rough for a soft voice. "I'm Johnny."

He too rough for a name like Johnny, too. A Johnny is a shy loan officer at the credit union. He come home with a box of chocolate just because, and help with chores. Bambi got the wrong kind of Johnny.

"I'm your neighbor over here." He point to his house. "Something happened the other night. My wife, such a stupid woman, she tripped and hit her head. Had to call the ambulance."

I wait for the part that got something to do with me.

"The cops got it in their head I done something to her. That it wasn't no accident." He take a step closer. His soft voice start to crunch like gravel. That sound more like him. "Been going around bothering people with questions. They come bother you?"

His stormy eyes rake me over. That look I know. I can guess what he got brewing behind 'em. I wonder, if he can guess what I got just inside this door.

"You some kind of mute or something?"

I'm some kind of fed up. I lean against the door, letting my left hand—the one with the better grip—slip closer to the only kind of talking I bet he understand.

"Look, I know one of them cops was over here too long for you not to be running your mouth."

Folks always seem to *know* something about me, without me saying nothing. They always know what to expect from people like me on sight.

"What I do with my wife is my business." He prop his foot on the threshold. "Ain't no nosy bitch, or no Mayberry cop, gonna tell me how to handle my house. You hear me?"

"I didn't catch that, Johnny." The good one come hopping up my porch. Chest puffed up, wearing a pair of Levi's with a hole in the knee.

"It was nothing, officer." Johnny's too soft voice is back. "I was just looking in on my neighbor."

"That right?"

Johnny stare down his nose at him, then look over at me. My hand stay on the shotgun.

"How's Rebecca doing? Heard they released her from the hospital." The good one look him up and down.

Johnny still ain't talking.

"Listen here." The good one take a step, put himself chest to chest with Johnny. "If I ever catch sight of you on this property again, my badge won't matter."

That must make some wheels start turning in Johnny's head, because he tell us both to have a good afternoon, and get off my porch.

"Good afternoon, Ms. Vincent." The good one give me a smile.

"Officer Miller."

"May I, come in for a moment?"

I straighten up. "I was in the middle of something."

He walk up to me, get close enough for me to smell his sandalwood cologne.

"If you worried about that shotgun you got by the door, don't be. Not here as an officer." He meet my eyes. "I just want to talk."

Whenever somebody say they just want to do one thing, they got a whole other thing in mind. Ain't no room in my life for other things. I'm about to tell him that, when Mrs. Bullard come outside. Before she can look across the street, I take a step back and open the door for the officer.

I shut the door and lock it, wishing I'd left him on the other side. He wander around my front room for a minute, looking but not looking. I tell him to have a seat, while I make some tea. He nod. But instead of sitting, he follow me to the kitchen.

I try to act like him being here don't make me feel all loose in my skin. He start picking up the mason jars on the shelves, reading each label like it's in another language.

"What's this one for?"

I glance at it. "It's good for hypertension."

"They make medication for that."

"Not everyone can afford the white coat."

His face flush, and he put it back. The kettle whistle. I put some Earl Grey in the teapot. While it steep, I warm up two tea cups with a bit of hot water. I remember the shortbread cookies I made yesterday, and put those on the table. I make his cup, two cubes of sugar and a dash of cream.

"You remembered." He smile at me.

I don't smile back.

He drink his tea, eat half my cookies. Still ain't said why he here. He can bring it up when he feel like it. Whatever it is he need to say is about a decade too late anyway.

He put his cup down, stare at his hands. I can see words building up in his mouth, making it hard for him to keep it shut.

"I'm sorry." He look at me so long, it start to hurt.

I don't know what to do with his apology. So I tuck it in the pocket of that little hand-me-down girl's dress.

...

The honeymoon's over. Took all of thirty-six hours for Johnny's softness to wear off. Now, he over there hollering about her ruining his best suit. I can't blame him. Seem like that woman burn everything she touch.

He storm out the house, and tear off in his truck, kicking dirt and gravel into the half-paved street. He'll come home after he's drank most his paycheck, and got some attention from a woman who always so understanding of what a man's wife done misunderstood.

I go get the picnic basket I used to bring Nicholas' lunch to the station in, make sure I got everything. Careful of the sagging second step, I make my way off my porch and across the little patch of balding grass that separate Bambi's house from mine. I set the basket on the worn welcome mat, and ring the doorbell.

"Johnny?"

Sound like she sitting right by the door like an obedient puppy. By the time she up and peeking her head outside, I'm on my side of the grass.

When I get back to my kitchen, my sometime pet scratching at the screen door. I open it enough for her to squeeze inside. We settle on the couch with a book and some wine to enjoy the peace and quiet I bought us.

...

There's a deer on my porch, carrying a picnic basket. I open the door for it.

"I believe this is yours." She hand the basket to me, her lips smile like they ain't sure how. "Johnny loved it. Kept going on about how it was the best pot roast and pecan pie he ever had."

She tuck her arm across her waist, let her eyes fall for a second.

"I let him believe I made it."

Bambi got a little sense. I glance in the basket. She done washed all my dishes. Deer got manners, too.

"I know who you are. Who your husband was." Her doe eyes find mine. "What did it feel like when you shot him?"

I watch her, until I see it. Something in her stare die a little. I wave her inside.

Guess I got a soft spot for Bambis, too.

A Surrealist Dictionary

AARDVARK: The long, intricately shaped glass tube used in the distillation of a widow's veil.

ABBREVIATE: An opiate derivative of tears.

ABLUTION: A rainbow reassembled inside a nightgown and used for starting fires.

AFTERBIRTH: A spark-yielding mist.

APHRODISIAC: Light given off between carnivorous plants as a form of communication.

AURA: A very dangerous species of moth attracted to human blood.

AURORA: Nocturnal animal similar to a jellyfish and noted for its high-pitched screams.

BICYCLIST: One of several long, white-haired creatures resembling Llamas that emit cooing, voice-like sounds.

BODICE: A prism used only in the dark as a weapon, and closely resembling a hunting knife.

BOAR: A vessel used for transporting reflections.

BREATH: Spoons repulsed by geraniums.

CABAL: A very fast vehicle powered by cocoons.

CHAOS: A fleshy, succulent fruit - the seeds of which are often used as umbrellas.

CORMORANT: Chemical found in the human body during moments of contentment.

CORONA: A wind-powered honeycomb.

CORPSE: A luminous green flower that reflects the moon.

CUNNILINGUS: The sudden metamorphosis of a chair into a great bird.

DANCE: An invisible doorway in a wall to which sleepwalkers are invariably drawn.

DESIRE: The glow of bathing lunatics.

DIAMOND: Nocturnal animal similar to a jellyfish, but much larger and more ferocious.

DIVINING ROD: A dangerous device used to attract stars for digestive purposes.

DREAM: A dress to which the eyes of bicyclists are attached; robe worn by messengers.

EEL: The corners of a room where the walls meet the ceiling to

form an escape route.
ELEVATOR: A soft, spongy mass that consumes its weight in gold.
EROS: A species of hunting dog with bright red feathers.
ESTROGEN: Wishbone used for rearranging constellations.
ETHER: Female reproductive organ.
FACULA: A large net used to catch enchanted stockings.
FEMALE: One of several species of fur-covered tripods used for stimulating rubies.
FLAME: A violin powered by the eyelids of sleeping girls.
FOETUS: Form of hysteria contracted while moving around in a solar eclipse.
GLANCE: A bitter tasting fungus often used for catching shadows.
GOWN: A joyful humming sound given off by spider webs during electrical storms.
GRACE: The art of luring ravenous dogs into a state of springtime.
GYROSCOPE: Human female milk-producing gland.
HEMOPHILIA: A very sweet herbal drug that causes spontaneous, Undirected human flight.
HONEY: A sexual perversion involving a dolphin and a pharmaceutical cabinet.
HOCUS POCUS: The buzzing sound that characterizes a flaw in the universe.
HYPNOSIS: Music produced when a chrysalis and a flame exchange places.
INCENDIARY: An obscene gesture or position with intent to elude color by emitting an inky, jet black substance.
INCEST: A psychology of the body based on the oysters of space travel.
ISOSCELES: Insects that gather to form a doorway in a tropical forest.
LACONIC: A vanishing cream.
LOOM: A golden dust used for hypnotizing wolves.
LUNATION: The sound of tongues caressing before eating fowl.
MASOCHISM: Sparks given off by oyster-beds when the tides come in.
MENSTRUATION: The sound produced when rubbing two swans together.
MIRROR: The stillness preceding a flash-fire that never arrives.
NEGLIGEE: A fly-swatter similar to a bee's nest and used to fend off an attack of pianos.
NEBULA: A psychological condition in which the very essence

of one's being feels constructed of sound, rather than flesh and bone.

PLEASURE: A sundial that uses the wings of bats to attract forests.

SADISM: Moments during the vernal equinox when sunlight turns into honey.

SEX: A small white furry animal that attracts windows.

SHADOW: A hairless mammal that generates rainbows instead of saliva.

SOMNAMBULISM: A cleaning solution.

SOLACE: A large triangular oven in which fighting wolves surpass the speed of light.

SOLSTICE: The luminous blue fog surrounding a human body when the mind is elsewhere.

STARLIGHT: Liquid used to power a whispering machine.

SWIMMING POOL: A kind of mist secreted by pyramids when fending off an attack of vicious glow-worms.

VESTAL: Bright yellow flowers that grow out of mummies.

VULVA: Wind chimes that use the bones of children.

WHORE: Apparatus for telling the future; similar to a tuning-fork.

X-RAY: A sewing machine that uses sparks instead of thread.

YAWN: A species of seagoing plant.

YGGDRASIL: A golden frog that howls during the full moon.

ZOMBI: A glass slipper.

27 – PRIYANKA NAWATHE
India

Crossing Fin Line

Drops of water splashed all around her as she jumped in puddles wearing her newest pair of bright red boots. She was five with a lilting laugh and cheeks just as rosy as her boots.
•

Playful like the fish in the sea, she twirled around in the pool, pushing and wading the water with natural ease. She was eight wearing the warm red swimsuit with tiny pink heart on her belly.
•

She plunged into the aquarium scattering crumbs around her feeding the dolphins gleefully rushing towards her. She was twelve wearing a red and black polka dot swimsuit happily dancing in the depths with her friends.
•

Glass shattered with pool of bright red liquid beneath her as she crashed out of the thick Plexiglas tank of fresh water spilling all around her. She was seventeen wearing a ivory black
leotard with her blood reddening the water beneath her as she lay still on the ground.
•

Memories. They were so elusive. There were days when they snuck up on her flooding her thoughts with a thousand different emotions. And then there were days when all she noticed was the bright red haze around her.
The puddles she had splashed in when she was five had been acidic. It had slowly begun sucking all the air out of her lungs. There she had been flopping like a fish away from home, alive yet not completely, not for long. She needed to survive. It was the only thing that mattered. It had to be done. She was brought to Syreni Horreum, a shelter known to few chosen ones concealed deceptively beneath the timeless Shedd Aquarium. She was placed in the Terraqua section, the water in it bringing life into her pale still body. As air reached her lungs — not lungs; they were gills — she splashed out in a pirouette jumping back into the depths of the pool that restored her life. That was the day that Terry Fisher died and the new Arielle Shedd was born.

Solaris

"Solaris" is a "fireside chat," a monologue, or rather, a dialogue—in any case—it is without a doubt, a conversation between more than one log.

1

a bridge between two winds, the sound of summer calling up the rest of the family. i've never reached the house i don't think, only in my dreams. the ocean is a magnetic field but the fires are not an illusion. they could be ice, that they could, however these winds turn to ash.

how many teeth were you in the beginning, when the house was first built?   the house has no time. it reflects itself. like the mountain.

a camera has two eyes, water like paper wearing thin over top soil.   firefly skulls, veins open like raspberry fields.

2

an age marked by the number of alleged laboratories a government drops from the top of capital city, a dream made of insipid wafers that taste like sundown. they're coming you know, coming for all of us—lunar pyramids with circus wheels, with no ceilings...
a mountain appears, and disappears. a door opens, and closes. a house is a home, and then not-home. water delivered directly to the house's doorstep. my name has no meaning. an engine made of thunder storms speaks to no one in two faces.
"a rainbow shot my wrist."
a blue star frozen above fire and blood. the underwater sun, the solar moon dressed with ice. blossoms of suicidal genesis, a gun too hollow, silence guarding the door of an unreachable dream.
an age marked by its journey, but only the time spent in the sun, and not the shade. rivers boil, a hi-hat carries its own weight. a house

of silver flame, the house of the burning giraffe. it's in my memory, however, you are not. where did you come from?

where did you think you were going? where fire is synonymous with blood. an archangel hung like a premonition. the desire to make haste and never wake up. i've been told by someone we both know...that the house and the mountain claim to be *identical*, or the same "thing", but my eyes are not available.

connecting the dots, putting two edges together the color of charm. the ego draws a character in a cartoon, plays a list of new facts on a plug-in flute.   'thou are a wretched puling fool', the room is so small. measure the length of one's reflection by the strength of one's teeth. a just fate, 'a whining mammet'.

3

the river runs red, but not with blood. i think i'm going home, asleep at the edge of the flame; a crate full of falling ends. a film shown in select theatres of my mind, a back up dancer for the Dread Pirate Roberts.

do you think the language will fit in there?

caution-tape around the chimney, the glorious history of the oven, caught on fire.

telemetric finalities, a should for the end of time—a choice floats around a Vedic text, *you're not the one.* there was at one time, another who sought out the analogical mountain. a perfect allegory for its own cave. have you been looking long? i have also heard from various sources in my head, that the house up on the hill is a *convenience store.*

that's electric, *still within my mind.* a firm grasp on everything that is not around me, that i do. a lilac blade named without a constellation. perhaps the moon was the one to hatch the first dragon, or the sun...*fire made flesh.*

i no longer believe in the necessity of (my) end, this place knows no beginning, either. time sees whatever it wants, the tangential point between two lighthouses, the house of dragons.

4

god fills out an application for a single cigarette, the dream shakes, gets reality to leave its feet. thru the window like a yellow moon, a candle floats away, the flame becomes weightless.

bogs planted like land mines along the laws of T I M E; translucent moons, falling eggs crashing on tops of mirrors. i've always thought the room too big. the hallway that hangs, draped around the aorta of a glass box. have you come for a new epilogue?

several miles on the decline, the house hides from its own reflection, a sprinkler jet stuck on a tree; the mountain's imaginary tooth. how does one measure the length of unborn dreams?

the Machine's dream machine: death seeks preservation, nothing left behind. the death and rebirth of Asuka; a red crucifixion without a hand in the dream. twelve thousand plates of admission go unrealized.

5

black moon kept on hold beneath the outer shadow, a cremated shell with no memory of a dream. everywhere i look the water keeps turning, an eye cutting between the clouds. how old were you when you were born? can you remember anything else?

has anyone ever come back?

none. all are said to have been lost in their dream, that they were. a ring for a reward, a flame for a dream, a life for a death. we say that they're "lost", but it's true, most burn alive before they realize what's going on, that they do.

6

the vultured corpse of a holy desert of red cathedrals in a black sea at an unfamiliar dawn, an angel the color of rain hand on the residual bangs of peripheral madness.

7

if i'm ever going to remember what it was like at the top of the mountain, the street lamps draw a curtain down the walk, illuminating the contours of the path as it makes its legs. as the shoulder rests, all available sight is rendered useless. textures begin to monopolize conversation, the veins of leaves are suddenly newfound linguistic currency. the language of stars has become no longer relevant, the stolen fractals bend the enigmatic radio waves like origami.

without *looking*, as one might with do with an eye, or a camera, symmetry has taken its place between both lighthouses, dancing up and down each wave in the water as it crashes and rejoins its ancestors.

8

never had a taste for the reflection, the peak rose to the occasion. full of never-ending films, acrobatic turnstiles, anti-magnetic allegories depicting laws ground in peradams; the courtesy of the rest of the island to never move more than one time remains the climbing soul's greatest triumph.
when i arrived i thought i had better take a mask.
a time series swinging back and forth on a rusted altar's dead weight pendulum, the natural light never quite hit the reflection of the trailer.
the oven speaks and no one listens.

an undiagnosed cycle of time, the fervent splendor teeming with responsibility, on the hook to remember memories, on the hook to capitalize on the absence of each passing window. the train no longer runs between here and there, the doors to the station boarded up with old and unused boarding passes. a heaven without a god, factotum.

9

the maze reaps the energy coursing thru the mountain. the hallway of the convenience store opens its mouth, allows the ancient wapati to take root in every cavity.
i used to fall down into the space between the drawer and the dresser, lighting matches with great invisible flames, holding my eyes in my hands to see what action found the world outside of my new flat.

a void warned of a tasteless soul, a figure stares at a painting on the side of a large granite plateau. a whirlpool like an attic fan reigns overhead, slowly time is being pulled in by its vortex. the wind running to the top of the sky, the dark, azure ceiling, filling its mouth with sun and wind. the genesis from which we are hurdled into phosphorescent vacuums and various pollen allergens, i remembers god called it the *"the obituary mambo."*

the final discovery was the first time anyone looked up into the sky at all.

they said it was like seeing a dream for the first time, or seeing yourself falling out of the stratosphere from a few miles away, not being able to see quite that far, but knowing for certain, it was you descending down the solar chute.

10

an old, fettered crow sits next to a small body of water, low in sodium.

11

the real mystery is not what one is thinking, but how the thought arrives in the first place. the shore has been picked clean, uncircumcised algae float in their own natural coffins on top of the waterline.

the water is still, not calm, but still, naked.

still learning how to breathe, the algae, in one last, grand attempt to resurrect itself, draws a transmutation circle, not unlike the one famously known for transmuting human lives into red stones, and dives into the eye of truth.

there are those that say the algae first grew to foment insurrection, mainly between the sun and wind—however, for what reason, and who they were sent by, we are still unsure.

the flaccid water begins to bubble small marble bubbles, sending short ripples to the deepest reaches of the pond. the universe is not empty, but it is. upon the majestic disappearance of the algae, the ripples in the water wade, and eventually fall asleep, the body of water once more, naked and unfrozen. inside an absolutely colorless void, the algae is presented with a set of human teeth and a large cornea, infatuated with the chlorophyllic laces of the algae.

there are two rather gigantic stone doors. on one door is the alchemical tree of life with twelve branches. on the other monolithic door, are three images set over one another, vertically, moving from bottom to top: an equilateral triangle with a series of small intersecting lines at the top corner of the triangle, giving it the resemblance of a mountain, next, above the peak of the mountain, an "8", and finally, above the mysterious numeral, is a wide, perfect circle.

the algae, unable to think, is abruptly ripped through the "8" door as it opens, by a thousand hands and eyes, devoured and digested by the jaws of time. the algae achieves nigredo and is regrown from the bottom up.

during the reconstruction of the algae, it is again transported back to its home on the pond. just as it had left them, the bay of coffins still afloat, the water in a deep sleep.
the algae drowns anyway, a lily freezes.

12

the old, fettered crow packs up its things, departs.

GASLIGHTER *a play*

Telling Time With No Mention of Taste: Act One

an invisible cave. a field with four cars arranged randomly across the sea.
high grass. a meadow. a living room, small, compact. inside a shed.

a repertory theater made out of lice and tapered suitcases with nowhere to
go.
cut diamonds inside a television made in the 1990's. magnavox.
a glass table with a volcano in the center. a tall-slender mirror to the left of
the
television's shoulder.

a frame of the universe on one of four eggshell walls. planets asleep in their
orbit.
a strand of bulbous xmas lights wrapped around the inner crown of the
room.
an illuminated necklace.

a bookshelf. half-empty, in its own lane.

           the road holds no place to go. no direction
      but the silence has never mirrored the lake or the fire above the water
          — a gun!

         lifting up the town, no wings. just the power of flight!
              again up and away you go!
     throwing dust in the wind. across the surface area of time.
          (shaking head) what a waste...

the world spins. doesn't stop spinning. it spins and spins and spins
        it winds up and crosses over, like a tornado meeting its death
           yeah...right. just like that...

a wish resembles what i eat for dinner every night
      a plate and a table.
        what a way to die, at night
     filling up empty laundry detergent bottles.
to carry water across the threshold.
      what a way to live, at night...
         the world isn't responding.
           — we better try back later.

electricity warms the earth. an ancient fire.
Olympus, but without the frame, or thunder.
take with us the anguish, the hands full of blood!
again with the dramatic exclamations—fucking can it.
the list goes on and on, but never slows down time.
a merry-go-round with fractured mirrors and full reflections.

you better watch out, you know. i've seen that white horse around
here, lurking in the shadows and the trees. it's watching us, that white horse.
you mean to tell me that the world has been eyeing Death all this time?
a car without a steering wheel seems like not a good idea
"the head cheerleader at the game of violence"

isolated alleyways, or hard drives
limitless transition, a release without nomad
a river! fresh locomotion!

the kind that follows the ranks of tradition, and never lets go of the rope
when   water wants to drown
an elegiac witness.
no—a dumbass.

just wait, castles will crumble. they already have.
have you *ever* been able to tell time?
how old were you when the machine was born?
that box is fucking empty!

a gold watch. an empty swimming pool.
red balloons popped under the weight of a vacuum cleaner
dusting. always dusting.

fallen out of occupancy
i feel like an unacknowledged vacancy
a never-ending story of read errors, Pan's fucking Labyrinth
hey—let's all relax.
deserts are caught by storms everyday, but no one seems to care
you mean the way one wakes up, right?
no. i mean the drought that find itself *too full* of water, and therefore
submerges   into the submarine hidden beneath the water-bed.
that's a slow dive.
that sounds terrible
yeah, wow,,,bleak.
— definitely v depressing

i mean i'm not trying to sound "dark" but ya know, i don't know, water's
crazy
        like a dream without a sleep-apnea machine
        a train without a breath
        a sun without a dial

cars carve out homes within the invisible caves and circumcise their young.
    one burns an effigy of two.
      — wait, what?
    i've a confession to make...
      i've never read pygmalion.
    how'd you know?
      um, because i told you that? remember?
    that was *you*?
          there's no way we survive this.
      the fire is too hot.
        the water too cold.

    oceans to fill with helmets
      colbat!
      — suicide!
navigators tame the wind and pray for an early curtain call
      then no one gets paid...
    you're getting paid?
          the one to wish away a year or two after they wake up
to act and to flee
      — to see and grow like a tree!
        to take the world!
      sea by sea!
          you have to stop. please, this is killing me.
a lesson to be heard, but never learned

        ...what a fucking disaster.

    the world with no will to sacrifice
    a claim made by an atheist
      you mean, plagiarist...

noon is far too long to ignore moonlight
      fasting, for an end to the book, an end to the story
      yeah, and which story is that?
        the one about the little girl who lived down the lane?
of course not that one.
      a film remembers its many past lives. it feels the snare crack
        and the bass fill

there's a story we ought to tell about ought
     hold out your hands...
       — feel the rain
the oil that spawns between gears, yellow eyes in the night
     look. just look down there! there's no place to go!
       the road just leads no where. no place.
yea but that's still an end. it's still a *sequence*.
     high in nutrition.
       this is some great shit
         — it's a fucking cigarette.

       there's no future in a memory
      but there is however a past, and a present
       only if you're wearing the right mask
    or night vision goggles
    or the eye of ra
    or ten dollar sunglasses

the feeling i get when i clean my feet and wash my hair
    an imaginary saturation with no leash
     I CAN SEE EVERYTHING!
       only if you're wearing the right mask
     that's not up to you
a map with more than one compass
    an inferior class of problem
       the kind that can't see without a mask
what are these fucking masks you keep mumbling about?!
    bobby killed mike. you wanna see?
i'm waiting to find the past
    you've lost it again? really?
well, i woke up again in the middle of the dream...
    what dream?
you know, the one with the mountain and the hotel
    i have no idea what dream you're talking about.
O sure you do!

an atom splits. boils in a pot, with cauliflower and asparagus.
     this dream of yours...does it actually have an end?
    i don't know! i've never gotten passed the point when i always
wake up.
     so how do you know you've lost your past?
are you saying the dream and my past are the same thing?
     well no, just that, your waking up might be the "real" end
      of the dream.
one burns an effigy of two.
    i'm confused...

the memory and the dream are the same.
the cloud marks its glass
feels like a window,
undresses.

For One Night Only: Act Two

a well. torrent. at the base of the great pyramid. the ancient pool.
down the corridor of time, world continues to spin, its bell rings.
the universe deployed to keep secret the cosmic convoy.

the grave of robinson jeffers.
sunflower blossoms haunting the coast line with their midnight eyes.
a landscape without end.

    buried in the eyes of marianne moore, metallic teeth shining in the
sunlight
        eyes buried in the downpour where no one lives
a cave hidden in the white isle, cliffs crowing when found murder
          i wear the face of the spider when its asleep
   too well have tomorrows spent money and time searching their own
birth
        an island! one's destiny following the ravine
          ...talk about silence. a murder!

    where statues of planets come face to face with their sculptor
      an alchemic elegy
         no road too neat to snow
      i hate to admit it, but this island is surrounded by water...
            — is that supposed to happen?
no one left to forget

      caught the left from a blind side

my drink turning into swan
    i scrape the shadow out from my eyelids
        rolling blossoms with their own petals
          — ripe to smoke
      bodies lay on backs of white serpents
      my favorite source of wealth
         how often do you actually iron your clothes?
       fold the grave up like an origami moon
         i am my own metal fish!

listening to my liquid gun call home
     the sparrow cut in by its gradient
          this doesn't sound like dialogue at all
    yeah, until you look up

        until the faucet curdles its drip

the calf drops off its milk before school
     the star that orders ice at the bar
        no, the flies don't find you attractive
    a perfect century
        such drama
     even a thousand seasons couldn't find a summer sun
well that's not like you at all...
      don't threaten *me* with a good time
    i can feel the soil drink in my skin
        turn me into leather
        peeling away flesh
      flame-broiled gold around the ankles
an ostentatious voyage
     there are great technicians that eat electricity
       —and time!
        pearls at the bottom of a wine glass
    a bottom
      cut from the neck of the top
        perfume in the leaves
where one day turns into two days
    rubbing my legs together like a cricket

     the music on mute

    like language tastes bars of february steam out of ears into bottled
night
     i can't count a single syllable
the wings too slow for the tongue
      a note pinned to the body of ovid
    putrid lemon
     — a solar deity
          fallen on the sword
     my breath, a hologram
    so cold, months have run out of calories
      a blue glass ball wrapped with a single piece of masking tape
the newspaper now made of analog clocks
    what time is it?
the river stolen my heat, and mirror

                    this is hardly the time for jokes
                ...head gathering steam...
                        fallen on the sword
        a conjurer
            a ticket!

dancing away with blades
                        what are you doing here?
        are we all awake? i know it's early
                    yeah yeah yeah, just get goin already
                            i don't want to get up.
        i know but we must. the sun has challenged us to a race
            where? it's like five a.m.
        it's coming along now, just wait.
                        this is fucking trash.
a world too young to know
            too young to know anything
— too young to know nothing
                        i am a cocoon.
        a tech fleece dream
                    where are we?

        the zoo stripped of its economy
            home absent in the shadow
i wander down the stairs in the morning and...
                        — hold my lungs in my hands!
i was going to say...and get a cup of coffee...
        i'll take one too, if you're goin. an extra shot pls
                    O yes me too! a mocha!
        i need an americano, two extra shots, with room
                frank and dale
wait what? no, im not going to get anyone coffee
                nope nope nope it's too late, you have to go now
and why's that?
            because it's your turn
                because you offered first!
                    look!

            — the sun is coming up!

        the thought had nothing to do with opposition
                let's be logical, yeah?
nothing to do with a flame
                my legs in a fire place.
        how do you prefer to cook eggs?
            your FAVORITE way to prepare them?

                        160

hmmm?
        a trilogy so old, the image has begun to fade away
        the ink drying in the well
bricks crumbling in the pasture
apartment windows nailed shut
    the thought had nothing to do with opposition
      free base in deadstock ticks
       i'll be waiting
the world in its final thought
       what do you think?
idol relics self-contained in their tombs
    wall to wall sales
hey, there's nobody on the phone?
       — and?
well why did you hand me the phone?
      TO CALL THE PLUMBER
ecstasy painted by a needle
    the world in need of a last leg
      spinning and spinning and spinning
asleep with my deathwatch
layers to be seen
      this is the wealth of the well
hearts on the screen
      a plumber to fix the pipe
we need the ink moving!
how old the number on the door,
the number of electricity?

      spelling out-loud names of numbers that can't tell time
quelling the calm of hyphenated phonetics
      — was that even a sentence?
      — sounded more like a reflection
more "journal" than "theater"
    let us all live truly terrifying lives
without aliases! or walls!
      or curtains made of cathodes
surely, the height of antiquity
    agreed, but don't—
      — nope, don't even say it.
but...
      nope. not a chance. absolutely not.

death is my favorite word
  — yeah, we know

    a kind of soft ray, or beam of light

161

branches with red leaves
revolutions around a star
ladders held together by magnets
taking turns climbing to the top
a world we cannot see

not a chance we can't see the ball drop
you're just a fly with no wings
a spider without a face!
clipping the promise made by the gun while you were awake
a skeleton with no bones
there's nothing to see here.

..is that it?

Eyes Without Eyes: Act Three

in a theater that dreams of being three theaters. a bug swats at a human.
there is a sun on the roof smoking a cigarette, on break.
fourteen graves dug out in the middle of the stage.
a couch. a bedbug hidden in the clouds.

a corpse asleep on the couch
with a book on their chest.

living under god i've always found a way to breathe
a snorkel really, calibrated to swim down the wind pipe
did you call the plumber yet?
yawning like these words make a difference
...do you mind?
poems like people
lost planets running sand bricks instead of heroin
the oven in not on
we are not doing the same thing

"mist or smoke
— on the bare high limits"
a spark underwater

overlooking the necessity
for warmth, and oatmeal
a variety pack
living between doses
never having been a fat cable, or a nose full of leather

the pharcydes, the curtains...
— stuffed in MY pocket like a handkerchief
my new sombrero
i like to suck on the artery
hibernation
two tones painted on a single wall
you're a pretty shitty graphic designer
— yeah it's not my forte
i keep a throat in my tomb
who are you, Juliet?
god of the "new" theater
an ugly god
— the divine marionette

...and who killed it...

the life of the party
taking off in a small batch of fuel
the terror always written in the face of prosperity
links to my at
the filler has never known a proper brine
...are you sure these are my lines?
yes now just keep going! go!

the world at its end
"where your condition has become serious and is reported on the radio"
hearing voices when i look in a mirror
pangs made of bronze
lavender sun flies poking holes in my sense of touch
a killer reflection
daffodils are my favorite kind of clock
this is how much i want to go to war
a fallen angel the color of time
Lazarus recited only in the morning
i'm afraid i've fallen in love with a dead lamp maker

— well that's certainly unusual.

swollen left to testify
waiting to digest an exit sign
a regenerative anti-biography
those willing to leave, keep up
liminal provisions
masses looking up at the bottom of the sea
who will you confide in?
dust to dust

— an opal graham cracker
dolling out on-screen vendettas
    "...the PEAKY FUCKING BLINDERS"
i'm high and disputing catholicism
    what a fucking square
    — a dodger dog!
  — oscar meyer!
    — an L seven weenie!
        dear god, please help me.
this is my favorite galaxy

god is full of milk!

the evening lays down its wings next to water
    pending authorization
  colloquial soundtracks measured by new eugenics
    an equal opportunity payout
calling on the stage!
    what stage, there's no stage here
  hiding in the plaza!
and lacking in silence.
    these jaws are from another country
you mean dimension,
    no, i mean country. a nation that has long since passed
i worry that your talking about us
  "what year is this?"
who are you?
    i come from a most golden company, a green spring
...
  ...
    what the fuck does that mean
yeah—what?
    the future. i'm from the future.
    just say that next time.

i live in a bowl that boasts bones like Alcatraz
    my brain asleep at the wheel
    what a race against time!
a heart too big to be hollow
    speed and its oldest memory
these bars are beginning to lose ink
    slow and steady
is this what patience feels like?

recover data
throw my glasses in the fire
this is getting ridiculous
always there to bring us down, aren't you?
you love to lick the glass box!
but it's my job...
fuck you, who cares!
the end is near
TAKE ME WITH YOU

it's getting warm in here...

Heat Death: Act Four

the world continues to spin on a frictionless axis. investigating imaginary
crimes and maintaining contact with the other dimension. the one across
from this one.
the dimension with the sun dial.

the meadow writes its past. never looking for a miracle. turning up soil one
handful at a time. the sun runs its finger over the spine of the blue car. the
sink lowers.

televisions float in with waves running up on the sand.
matching screens, salt around the remote lids.
the shed, calm.
smoke rises.

a category four tornado
a living command of water
taking in the cynicism of a rained cause
burn the lilies
the brain in the heart stem!
the trachea?
no no, the voyage!
charred seasons
my shoulders turn in the wind

fallen away with the memory of silver bells
looped around a lunar metronome

see that black smoke?
it means they're coming, back
who's coming back?

they are coming back.
...and who's this "they?"
the first clocks, the first seasons
the head of the snake!
lithographs printed in tempura
phone booths filled with boiling red water
sharpening the midnight stroll
— toll!

the work has oft been set against itself in the middle of the equation
just say "often" next time
another day goes by while grammar loses its teeth
the change is nowhere to go or see without a place to see
i'm going fast to sleep in the whim around on the mill
grass bent in the light
another "home"
time left without a memory to dream about
calling off work to dream
catch a fish!

a lasting impression with undivided attention
kept thru these phases like moons
a draft bleeding through the cracked window
no mist left to memorize
death is all i see
tell time
can a clock measure space?
no

odd definitions written with both hands
"the pearl in the depth of future centuries..."
nothing cut but the claim
filed at the last minute
the nation's health insurance revoked
yards covered in Blue Roses
i am a voice!
these are the emeralds.
and this, the painting.

the story of the red car that lost its garage
the apocalypse, but with yeezus playing
earth wrapping itself in a blanket of magnets
— death's love letter!
— love's death letter

in the courtyard with the plotting sunrise
"like particles drunk on butterflies
— fragrance

...solitude"

these last few scenes haven't been very much fun

i feel that we've been betrayed by our creator
yeah?
how's that?
is telling time a crime?
who is this creator again?
i mean to say, i am sad and this is bullshit.
O such a change of heart!
a body in the sea!
that was brutal
i dream of throwing the moon at the sun
no quarter!
walk the plank!
planting indigestion in the soil
watching the earth grow
back to the meadow and the graves
the pilot with kerosene wings
frosted trees looking for their frozen leaves
this is the sand
— and this is the river.

operation overglow
Machamp uses "seismic toss"
the engines squeal in traffic
automated torture!
born in valleys of Neptune
BROADCAST VOCALS ON UNSUNNY BROADSIDES
north of the vat of radiating particles
time to test my bedside manner!
an equal tragedy
lifting the grass from its bed
surging thru the planetary veins
our last breath of formlessness
i'm not very good at this!

drunk in the packet-boat
down 3-1 to thermodynamics
an education cauterized by irons in twilight
dreadnaught!

"the summer demands and takes away too much"
in one flash a distant memory
            another tunnel at the end of the light
water and the faucet
        — *the infernal machine*
     one last glass of "night..."
        there's fire rising over horizon!

29 – ADAM ROOKE
Ireland

Lungbutter

see-through fingers
through the breasts, the ribs

buds, flower heads bent
on the wilt, unclipped
and cupped last night
you rubbed butter from the lung
in with the blunt of your thumb

to shine yourself up
like hair through a comb.

It looked like asthma,
it looked like a struggle
but it wasn't.
I asked you to take the wasted spaces,
the neck I breath with.

We share a breath,
we don't waste it talking.

USA

The following two poems are from a sequence that is a constraint-based erasure produced from the text of Dylan Evans's Introducing Evolutionary Psychology. Every chronological page was treated as if it was a word bank for making each line. The title of each section is derived from the subtitles on the pages that correspond to the pages used to fashion the section.

Reciprocal free-rider exchange

Help return the biologists. Call a risk
the strike of a hungry member. The precious

scientist worked to be treated repeatedly.

The cohesion of strategy answered
the hominid face. We tally fifty ancestors

and propose trading.

Donors on the range.
All these reciprocal, true animals

parenting into intensive old age.

The unit of kingdom is a replica of kind if
the coefficient is coined by a shared common.

The cost of relatedness stands to rule.

The truth about nepotism

Close mechanisms predict
step-parents set points

that rarely lower. Looking

for a channel about Canada
with limited food raises risk.

Decisive machinery take children

to want the lies of the crux. Sisters,
illustrate a cake to 100%. Divide

no milk forever. Time to gain from the same

The following two works are constraint-based erasures. The source text is Dylan Evans's Emotion: The Science of Sentiment. Each sentence is derived from a (chronological) page of the book as if the page were a word-bank (with the exception of the italicized "programmer" speaker in "THE COMPUTER ~~THAT~~ ~~CRIED~~," whose words are derived from the same page that was used to compose the previous sentence). The poem titles correspond to ("edited") chapter titles.

THE COMPUTER ~~THAT~~ ~~CRIED~~

Programmer, who is Robin Williams, and might I play with him? *When the humanoid is dry, implant.*

I prefer to fix primitive people—but shouts I like not; the clever fake a bridge with straitjackets. *The tide is an essential critic.*

We hit mental economy with the pointless, facial narrowing. *We are the sine qua non contemporary philosophers.*

>

One element inclined—now I think: are we parochial to say their brains are bizarrely furry? Most computers do not possess chauvinistic sweating; however, circuitry stands on end, behaving on the hair, developing, tending to the brain as if native.... But the synthetic of the head!

Humans are surely guilty of anthropocentrism, but doted machines on desks, modulating the nonlinguistic to be able to voice? I, the size of a bump, infer I sound not so good. Anthropomorphism has me, and it headed off.... Flight of fancy passwords.

Humans proposed; computers propose better. Wearable computers involve giving a human holes; I am not luxury. Split-second hands-off micro-surgery search-and-rescue was the beginning. Clever, the right amount of benign, the computers conducted wisely.

A mood may build up in the full-blooded, and we interrupt the neurobiological keywords. Rapid highlight of envy, and algorithms for love shoot the emotion like spacecraft. These are simple programs for improving kids, babies, pets. Their minds are not filled with the grim—subservient they; nuclear missiles not needed. However, are we not violent?

Computers and people are predictable, deliberately creep, erase, occupy, all to have imperfect life. Lies in the materials, the code, the chromosome: there are no protagonists. Populations copy until filled with viruses. Consciousness lacking room; zombies by essence.

The armed carry out rules, but the rules are computer inscriptions. Better that the far-fetched disk become salt. Our lives link to capacity. Salvation is to not exist.

THE HEART HAS ITS REASONS

One hot gut consults danger and calm, and jumps to court, concentrating *flee* to logical show; it is not just to do traditional nothing. For example, creatures of motto are silly and overestimate their familiar choice, even making the devil seem pretty; better to have several alternatives between two cities of exposure.

Inflated lucky prizes go off, over-optimistic, wasted on attracting partners; better to drive away, not be in a line of people, these paradoxical exhibits you pay to trust.

A good gut outweighs the con artist—that trump-face, holes cheaper than the ground's detriment; a creature writing is not a press—lacking balance and blinds.

A set of economists, roughly out of step, seem crazy to want the world, not because the world wants to rest, but because there is no such thing as a consumer's heart—I think that the last question speaking from a well is a sensible good. Our given ends achieve first place for enlarged calling.

31 – VERÓNICA CABANILLAS
Peru

La vida es un trueno que galopa sobre un caballo enloquecido.

Me choca la vida como un trueno galopante en mi corazón

Y empiezo a volar con dos mástiles atados a la tierra

Un arpón me cruza el pecho

Y toca el cielo

La vida la veo fragmentada, como en escenas fugaces donde el

agua se deshoja

Y me veo ascender o caer, es lo mismo,

Sobre el atardecer de la pintura que aprieto incesante

Y en el fogón la quemo con mis manos hasta verla renacer ante la

inquietud sofocante de las ventanas

La vida es un trueno que galopa sobre un caballo enloquecido

Que bebe de día y de noche

A punto de dormir sobre el regazo de mis soles

Veo los días que vienen

Veo sus rostros

Dormirse en mi pupila

Veo como el cielo se abre

Los sueños se descifran y se deshacen en la punta de mis labios

Es la sal

O la humedad

En las vías negras

de quienes amo

Sus voces y sus tersos cuerpos amotinados

Unos sobre otros en forma de montaña

Atravesada en el medio por esa vía que me encanta recorrer

De ida y de vuelta

Pararme y sentir la brisa desahuciada de los locos

Y así mirar hasta perderme

En la letanía

Aquellas luces que se demoran

Cantan todos los finales y los ciclos en que la vida se sumerge

La fiebre se eleva y es momento de vivir

Un día

Sin resplandor

Sin miradas

Sin voces

Solo uno con los brazos en alto

Grita su llegada.

32 - STUART INMAN
UK

The Dead Way (From REMORA)
(Have you ever danced with the devil and laughed in his face?)

I.
A ribbon in my bones

The stone path
A torn sky like a purple robe

A path of dancing bones

The light froze and fell to earth

Clotted perfume
Veil of shimmering bones

Toothed libidinal

These my living masks

II.
The river is a knot
Glass flesh twisting upon itself

The path is a vapour
Chimerical

The bone-yard is a sanctuary
For the flayed

III.
For the silent hours
The sightless vigil
The black and white mask

IV.
Broken bread broken stones
The way of knives and bare feet

Of ice in the heart
And a black sun in the head

Cramping and phantasmagoria vacation

In summers of active cramp
Drift fragments and frozen
He never took off on the beaches
and broths deviate from your board.
Sandy shores
From the shroud in walls.

Go to your king's figures
Sandblasted rounds
Security in rooms
Image of your self
In greedy brain winters
Reactivate feelings and roofs.

Never made snowman in snow
And sleds disappear from your curve
Redomas in the mist
Pathetic phantasmagoria in
fireplaces
Serum, candle width
Fog in the dome
Insular allegory in woods.

34 – PETER HARRIS
UK

THE BLIND WATCHMAKER

In my fingernail I see the universe, forgotten planets and grains of sand,

I see a black lake in an arctic storm where winds ruffle the feathers of green swans and the cold touch of a stranger makes my spine shiver with pleasure,

like the taillights of cars on a night-time freeway.

Put me in the hands of the crippled carpenter still wearing his lipstick and coat of grass and let me lie in the deserted quarries.

Warm me by the embers of fires left by travellers and meteorites,

fill my stomach with soil and leaves and place birds' eggs in my empty eye sockets.

Roll me in sea foam and let me speak to the creators of emptiness

Let my body grow beneath the fungi.

Do not pity me.

I have painted walls with the looks from your eyes and danced to the songs of the violin player who stands behind the morning,

I have shuddered between your breasts

And felt the mountain's red mist on cliffs of chalk,

Bathed in waterfalls of ermine.

No more the fool.

No more the executioner.

No more the colours.

Only white.

White like laughter.

White like the forgotten child.

White like a distant voice beneath the icy waters.

White like the kite of probability.

This is the domain of the blind watchmakers.

35- SEAN NORTHRUP
(1949-1997)

PARADISE IS JUST...

Disturbed during the soup;
A white glove on a black marble table,
A street after the rain.
The torn body, whispers, come,
With your toilet singing;
"I am eating as if I were already dead."

The clock, its arms around the room;
Staggers an armchair,
Shed slowly into a pigsty,
Trail of tears, a crown of bees,
A cloak of grass.
Alice in Wonderland!

Clouds, poetry hand cranked jam wheels; hardly standing, the radio bleeding.
Sovereigns from their crabbed fingers, its nails, Love before War.
The birds outside hold back madness with their wired eyes.
Sheets have already thrown up their stale supper.

Statues - Mud is slinging religion tins to three chords,
The parlour is empty, the guests, All Vacuum:
Another wheel,
Milk tastes like marble skin.
The bread, hymns to blacked out windows.
AGAINST

GOD.   DEVILS.   like wine
                                    like velvet
                                            like snapshots
                                            like old leaves,

Suits with arms, line, empty trains,
the pox, stale lips,   like flesh,
                          like cups,

ART -   garret, parades,
            unprovoked silence. Harmony, junk.

WORK

Under finger-nails – gob; Trash, pinned, stripped, gumless, makes, Suicide – Sinks.
The dignity of labour:

                The dignity of labour:

The fall of Christ, kicking thighs, its tongue through stone, through wood.
Wheels crossed, Jesus wept, his burning violin; swans to water, to Eagles swirl.

AGAINST

Avenues, shades, newspaper flies, tributes, a universe of books,
On the habits of chairs. Money. Foul singer starving the living,
Old whore; The death of Ivan Illyich.
Two and Two make five a reality. Sculpture, Drawers, filled with black light,

            unconscious language,
            uneven earth,

                A new headstone
You've heard about Jerusalem;
The feeling one's head is exploding with......
Smooth Rolls Royce
The heady concoction.......
Slashing and sucking at the wound,
We call it ....the skull.

Relentless piece of near-blasphemy,
We could hear all most nothing
Of the world outside.
Sleepwalker.

Read about it, talked about it.
It sounds in silence, but it cannot relieve it.
Bamboozle.

Blackshirt after the wedding feast,
(The feeling one's spine is drilling into the brain)
The arms of Christ are spread out.
Sulphuric acid over Venus.

ARE WE MAD?

Between the skin and the flesh,
Eases his fingers forward.
Pains in the head..................flashes.
Stretch your legs,
The earth darkens.

 "When we got tired it felt
As if we were painting the side of a mountain!"

No noises, no footsteps.
The bloodiest war in history.
(shakes his head) it won't wash;
At the next table.......

WESTERN SLUMP

Happy, smiling inviting.

"Paradise, is just..........

"The feeling that a whole layer of skin has been ripped away.

36 – ROWEN FOSTER
USA

I'm Sorry
—after Ben Mirov

I'm about asleep after three. My plans fall in shadow. Sorry about my dirty t-shirts, the drinks I smashed. I have an hour to sit in a park. Someone grabs my hand, their shadow, a ghost. The park in shadow. We meet for three hours. The kids crush their homework. Their little hands dirty. I'm sorry. The kids crush me. Their little hands grab me. Three drinks in my throat. My throat falls asleep. After the ghost sits we have to hand in the plans. The plans for the kids. My little *dolores* sit in my throat. I'm in shadow. Your hands fall asleep. I'm sorry you're sorry. I'm sorry I smashed your plans. I'm sorry after an hour. I'm sorry about the drinks. The kids fall asleep. In the park, I sit in dirty t-shirts. My hands crush the ghost. The ghost in my shadow. My hands grab my throat. The hour falls asleep.

37 – MAX CAFARD
USA

Times Tables

Please memorize the following multiplications for the test:

1. pincushion X muffin = larva

2. hot air balloon X mice = cotton candy

3. swordfish X thunderbolt = growl

4. camera lens X milkshake = gondolier

5. galaxy X garbage can = bullfrog

6. panic attack X flour sifter = ogre

7. flimflam X pencil sharpener = window washer

8. indigo X tennis = skeleton key

9. return trip X bellyache = wow

10. fingerprint X blink = glacier

11. celery X sand dune = punch line

12. palomino X mischief = semi-colon

Good luck on the test, students!

Sincerely,

Your Teacher

38 - BRANDON FREELS
USA

I'M REALLY SCARED WHEN I KILL IN MY DREAMS
SHE IS NOT ALONE

I was looking for some kind of turtle along the rocks of a seaside cliff. At the top there was a girl who claimed to be the turtle I was looking for. Afraid of heights, I suggested we find a place at the bottom of the cliff where we could make love. But when we began to climb down she became tense, afraid that after making love she would no longer be able to climb back up. Instead she took me to a hole not far from the edge of the cliff. Inside the hole there was a house with a flat roof. It was missing several walls, and a small wooden fence surrounded a part of the porch where the girl said she slept. In the yard there were several empty flowerpots, and a blanket had been spread out over the body of a black lab. I noticed some swollen legs peering out from behind the walls. The girl told me they were the legs of her dead mother.

PROTECT ME YOU

When I was seven I was possessed. I later learned that it was the spirit of my grandfather, but at the time I didn't know what was happening. I began shaking violently and was unable to sit still. Even when I was not trembling on the outside I could feel my body moving on the inside, like a marble spastically bouncing on a roulette wheel. All the people in the my neighborhood came to watch me shake. My mother told them I had just eaten too many hotdogs. Once I ran out the door, towards the river, and when they caught me I suddenly started shivering. I was clutching a drawing of some kind of fish with a lion's head. When taken home I was given some milk and a sandwich.

I LOVE HER ALL THE TIME

There was no one in the library. We walked up the stairs to the top floor, and she pointed out a cluster of strange roots piercing through the ceiling. Water slipped from them, creating small puddles on the floor. I got down on my knees and started lapping up the water. She

186

had no problem reaching the roots themselves. I watching her as she swallowed the water, her thin neck rhythmically dragged the water down her throat. A funny feeling came over me, and I found myself under her long hoofed legs, thinking about how easy it would be to climb up them and inside her. Her tail fanned my forehead, a gesture of some kind. She spoke in snorts and coughs, and while I couldn't understand her most of the time, I knew that she was on my side. The water dripped down her throat, her chest, her cunt, her legs, to my mouth, to my tongue.

SECRET GIRLS

In grade school a group of older girls took me to a network of natural caves beneath the school's basketball court. Inside they forced me to take off my clothes and kiss their bodies in inappropriate places. When the fat one stuck her fingers in my mouth I got scared and ran. In a panic I lost my way, and stumbled onto a path made from smooth stones. The stones led to an entrance that had curiously been blocked with some kind of sludge. After removing a small portion of the sludge I squeezed passed and into the next chamber where I found, in a small pool of water, a broken statue of a girl. The statue was shattered into several large pieces. A small plaque nearby said it was the likeness of the nymph Salmacis. Slightly beyond the statue, towards the rear of the chamber, was a wall covered with large, energetic wasps. Barely visible because of the wasps, I noticed another statue halfway submerged in the wall. I began beating the wasps with my jacket, but they soon covered my body and I fainted.

PACIFIC COAST HIGHWAY

When I was seventeen I tried to drown myself, but instead I simply floated. Where the Columbia and Willamette rivers meet I was abducted by a school of salmon that pushed me into the ocean. I drifted through tornadoes, occasionally was run over by boats, and was even chewed on by a few sharks, until finally I washed ashore on an island occupied by pigs. "Who are you?" a gray pig with one tusk asked, "We did not call you." The pigs began eating my flesh. "Chop off my head," I cried, "boil me if you must, but please do not abandon me on this island." After a long deliberation the pigs left, swimming out into the ocean like a pack of seals.

TOTAL TRASH

The bus left me on a corner I had never seen before, near the long grass of a country graveyard. I was not a man, but something dark and horrible to live with. One of the graves looked as if it had been tampered with. An orange extension cord rose from it like a discolored whisker. I followed the cord out of the grave and into the backyard of a decaying house where it descended into the soiled water of the house's swimming pool. While pulling on the cord I heard some dog's barking on the roof of the house, but I couldn't see them. In the pool I noticed something large moving, shaped like a guitar yet alive. It was attached to the cord, and the more I pulled the more it pulled back. At some point I walked into the house and found a sheet of maggots covering what once could have been a cat. One of the dogs was sitting by the stairway, as if it was guarding it. The house stunk of fish. Fur covered everything. In the kitchen was the body of a man who had shot himself in the face. There was a glass of milk on the table and an empty bowl. He was wearing some jogging shorts and Converse shoes. There was some oatmeal on the stove. All the clocks in the house had stopped except for his watch, which rested with his arm on the kitchen floor, both covered with teeth marks.

ECHO CANYON

I was on my knees, my mouth rubbing against her cunt, when I turned my head and became dizzy. Her face was dark and long like an Egyptian pharaoh. When I was with her I had a tremendous desire to love and be loved. Her lips looked as if her own teeth or someone else's had chewed them off: dry and rough. I fearfully refused to touch them with my tongue, but I wanted to. We were hiding behind a large boulder when I heard the church bell ringing. It stood out, even above the wind, like a cancerous mass. In the distance I could see one of the priests. He was wearing a white gown and carefully coming down the canyon trail. Behind him was a large white cross with wheels attached to it. "Brandon," he shouted, after spotting me, "I've brought you some food." When I didn't answer he continued shouted, "Brandon, I love you like I love all my friends!" Grabbing a large rock I quickly ran up to him and slammed the rock deep into his throat. His body shook violently for several seconds, sending out blood in all directions before lapsing into a calm repose. She walked up to his body, removed his bloodied gown, and placed it over her naked flesh. "Brandon," she said, "I love you like I love all my friends!"

PIPELINE

Looking into his hole was like looking into the void. I began stuffing my hand into it, then my arm. I was sure the others had come out to the poolside, watching us in their magnificent costumes: one as a bullfrog, another as a potted flower, a third as a diving bell. I was able to fit my second arm into him and finally my head. His body was much bigger on the inside. After slipping into him entirely I waited to be born again. It was like being trapped at the bottom of a well. For days I did nothing but touch the walls around me, feeling him through the darkness. Without warning, a crack of light appeared, and a massive flush of water was expelled from his body, taking me with it. I awoke in the desert, stinking of vodka. His body was next to me, but it looked empty, limp. Several feet away an old woman was playing a biwa and singing in Japanese. She paused momentarily: "He is no one," she said in English, "He is anyone." The worst thing about surviving are the memories that survive with you.

DISAPPEARER

Deep in the pit I could still remember her face. Like a dead pig she covered my fat body with hot dirt and rocks. The rocks had strange symbols on them, and words written in a language I couldn't understand. Under the heat my body whimpered and whistled. Sulfuric steam shot out of my nostrils, and my feet grew thick, like an elephant's. My hands became swollen roots, searching the soil for something moist to take in. The hair on my body grew long and bountiful, covering every inch. My head ached as it slowly took on the shape of a long, piercing object. After three months this new form caused my head, now a great horn, to protrude from the earth and into the hot summer air. Through it I could finally feel the wind again. I crawled from my grave a helpless, deformed thing. A boy in a baseball uniform ran to me, and asked if I needed assistance. But my new horn, with one quick instinctual stroke, cracked his skull open before I had a chance to respond to his generosity. I took the boy's body to a nearby barn, and ate it.

DREAMS OF LAW
from THE PRINCE'S TOMB

Prince Shotoku Taishi (572-622) was the legendary hero who, at the beginning of literacy in Japan, made Buddhism and Confucian governmental principals two of the foundation stones of Japanese culture. He wrote the earliest commentaries on Buddhist Sutras and commissioned the first histories in Japanese. He is also credited with beginning the traditions of Noh theater, archery, tea Ceremony, sculpture and architecture, among other cultural forms

I
1.)
Alone in the Hall of Dreams, Shōtoku Taishi read from a text by Hsun Tze.

"When the sage kings instituted names, the names were fixed and the elements of reality were thereby distinguished.
The sage kings' principles were carried out and their wills understood.
Because they were carefully led, the people were unified.
They did not follow promiscuous nomenclature and were not deceived.
When words and things are thus bound, influence and achievement represent the success of government."

2.)
Some days later, in the palace garden beside a pond, Prince Shōtoku Taishi conversed with Empress Suiko. It was evening. Oil lamps had just been lit. He read aloud from texts the Chinese ambassadors had brought.

"The King of Cheng wished to write down the laws and punishments in his domain and proposed having them cast in bronze on new offering cauldrons. His ministers opposed this. They argued that when laws were written, people would no longer cultivate virtue in their hearts but would merely obey rules because they feared punishment. Further, peoples' minds would turn to finding ways of circumventing the laws for their own advantage.

"The King did not accept the arguments of his ministers and he became the first ruler to write down the laws and the punishments for violating them. Ever since that time, Chinese rulers have charted their course between the poles of ruling by law and punishment and ruling by encouraging the cultivation of virtue."

The Empress thought before replying:

"How ancient this kingdom, that it knows the beginnings of things. China knows the moment when words divided the world. Words gave precedence to men's needs; they shaped and reshaped the shadows of the past. Virtues that were our innate inheritance succumbed to the power of the word to define and redefine them. Only words could aspire to permanence."

"For this reason," the Prince said, "Despite the risks, we should write down a code to guide our people."

The Empress agreed. "But will such a code be a shadow ruler, a secret Emperor or Empress. Will it move the hearts and arms and legs of people from the hidden domain of words?"

3.)
Alone in the Hall of Dreams, late at night, Prince Shōtoku felt a sudden chill. He thought he heard a voice whisper:

Around me, broken
They rest in the ashes
They, in tens of thousands,
The vanquished.

The dead have entered the dark world.
The living are uprooted.

The earth is gray.

II
1.)
Now there are no rules.

The city is bombed to wreckage, flat. Scattered here and there, teetering walls where once were government offices, temples, libraries, houses, gardens, roads and lanes. There are no roads, just a gray flat expanse, interrupted by heaps of bricks, broken chimneys, broken roofs, blackened trees.

A ghostly swirl of wind rises into the air and spins a piece of roofing metal in a whirlwind of dust. The acrid burnt smell makes his eyes water.

2.)

Nothing is left. War is over. He stumbles north, passes other soldiers searching for home, staring into empty space. No one knows what to do. The violence, the final destruction, has erased their sense of direction.

In the lunar landscape of destruction, he sees phantoms bundled in rags, sitting beside guttering bonfires, pawing through dark heaps of trash. Candles flicker in hovels; wisps of smoke trail listlessly from rusted chimneys.

Small spheres of pale blue light drift in the mist. Some rise, spin and grow brighter, others fall and fade in the cold night.

He is afraid. He lies by the road, sleeps. In dreams, the world still calls to him.

3.)

His family home, their shop, the road that led to it, the trees, there is not even rubble. Gray silky ash blows across what was once a city but is now was a flat desert of dirt, clouds of dust rising, the smell of corpses and charred wood. On a broken wall, the black shadow of a running man.

Stragglers, also in tattered uniforms, look around. They cannot absorb it. There are no more landmarks. He thinks he hears singing. He looks and blinks.

4.)

There is no place to live and nothing to eat. People live in holes. They are always dirty. They can't wash their clothes. They smell like animals. They cannot escape the smell of feces and urine and rot.

Many are sick with cholera, typhus, TB. Many will soon die. More will die starving. They can think of nothing but eating and eating and eating But there are no homes and nothing to eat. The Emperor cannot save them. Buddha cannot save them.

5.)
The blazing sky has touched the pale earth.
Eyes are scorched.
Words have no meaning.

The white disc of a single cloud
Hovers in the pale sky.
Flocks of sparrows wheel in the air.
Nowhere to land.

6)
He is wandering through fog. He thinks someone is talking nearby. No one is there.

III.)
1.)
"There's something you must see", his grandfather said long ago. "There's something I have to show you." The moment still was vivid. He was a boy. His grandfather turned and shuffled into the rear storage-room. He made his way to the back where puppets accumulated by generations of puppeteers moldered in the dark. Furthest to the rear were the oldest. The family never looked at them, but could never throw them out.

The boy never went there. The room had a strange smell of mold and sweetness.. The family had abandoned puppetry. His great-grandfather opened the grocery store in what were then the outskirts of Nagasaki. It soon became a prosperous suburb. His grandfather never let them get rid of the boxes of puppets.

He followed his grandfather and helped him retrieve the large black lacquer box from a high shelf in the very back. Dust filled the air. His grandfather couldn't stop coughing, but managed to say: "This, this is our beginning".

2.)
In an ancient cedar chest with rusted hinges, broken lock, there were eight lacquer boxes, each eighteen inches long, six inches wide and deep. All were battered, corners chipped, lids cracked. The boxes

were marked in faded gold calligraphy: 8) Text, 7) Knowledge, 6) Justice, 5)Loyalty, 4)Decorum, 3)Virtue, 2) Benevolence, and 1) Heavenly Appointed,

As his grandfather opened the boxes before him, one by one, each emitted a distinctive scent. 1) burning iron; 2) myrrh, 3) cloves, 4) cinnamon, 5) cardamom, 6) frankincense, 7) peony, 8) Iris and 8) camphor. He was 8 years old, but did not forget.

3.)
He remembered a song his grandfather used to sing:

"I have been away so long.
The paths are gone.
A thousand miles without chimney smoke.
I think of the house I lived in all my life.
I turn inward.
Alive or dead,
I cannot speak."

4.)
Eight black lacquer boxes: One contained a small worm-eaten sheaf of notes.
seven each contained a puppet about a foot tall, with a central rod to hold it, 2 thinner rods to move its arms. Each was lying swathed in raddled yellow silk. 6 puppets were dressed as courtiers.
7th black lacquer box, inscribed in faded gold: KNOWLEDGE. Puppet had a smooth blank white lacquer face, no eyes, nose, mouth, ears, white lacquer hands, wore copper hair ornaments, a black cap, and emerald green robes.
6th black lacquer box, inscribed in faded gold: JUSTICE. Puppet had a smooth, blank white lacquer face - no features, white lacquer hands, wore white cap, silver hair clips and deep blue robes.
5th black lacquer box, inscribed in faded gold: LOYALTY. Puppet had a white featureless lacquer face, white lacquer hands, wore silver hair clips, yellow cap and scarlet and dark blue robes.
4th black lacquer box, inscribed in faded gold: DECORUM. Puppet had white lacquer face, no features, white hands wore gold and silver hair clips, red hat with peacock feathers, and deep scarlet robes.
3rd black lacquer box, inscribed in faded gold: BENEVOLENCE. Puppet, white lacquer face, no features, white lacquer hands, dressed as a courtier with gold hair clips, green cap with leopard tails and lilac purple robe.

2nd black lacquer box, inscribed in faded gold: VIRTUE. Puppet- white lacquer face, no features, white lacquer hands, gold hair ornaments, a purple hat and purple robes.

1st lacquer box was red cinnabar inscribed in faded gold: HEAVENLY APPOINTED. Puppet slightly larger than the others. A gold lacquer face with no eyes ears, nose or mouth. Gold hands. Wore the gold crown of a Chinese Ruler with seed pearls hanging before his face and a yellow brocade robe adorned with dragons. The box contains 17 tiny paper scrolls.

They were very old. Costumes still vivid, ornaments bright.
Absence of nose, eyes, mouth makes the images prehistoric, ghostly, unsettling. Courtiers' faces were smooth as white porcelain. Each seemed waiting to assume the specific character that a future age would project onto him.

Larger puppet, Heavenly Appointed. His gold face was an immovable mask. Beneath it, a real character could never be seen or known.

As he unwrapped them, his grandfather seemed nervous. "My father, he only showed them to me once. We were changing the store rooms. He didn't let me touch them. It was late at night and I was tired, but I remember what he said: 'They look like dolls. But they move between the worlds of death and life. They move between past and future. It is their function. They are not human, but they are, in their way, alive, and waiting.'"

5.)
His grandfather laid out the boxes containing the puppets, opened them, removed the worn silk coverings. He did not touch the puppets nor would he permit his grandson to do so.

"No. We cannot. They are from a time we do not know. They communicate something we may no longer be worthy of."

But, when his grandfather turned away, the boy reached out and touched the forehead of the golden effigy. He could not understand. It was as warm as living flesh. Shocked, he pulled away.

"What did you do?"

"Nothing."

"Did you touch them?"

"No.... I promise."

His grandfather said: "I will show you these puppets as my grandfather showed them to me, and his great grandfather showed them to him. In that grandfather's great grandfather time, the puppets were already ancient, but it was six generations ago when they last appeared in performance. The words had all been memorized and passed down from father to son, so the scroll here consists only of notes. He read aloud slowly.

"As I understand it, these puppets were made almost five centuries ago. They were taken to Hokkaido when our people finally subdued the Ainu and took control of the entire Island.

"The commander of those forces, Takeda Nobuhiro, leader of the Matsumae clan, had a dream. He dreamed that Prince Shōtoku Taishi descended from the High Plains of Heaven with his entire court. He heard melodies and harmonies of a music he had never before heard. He woke suddenly, pulled back the screen, and looked to the East where the sun was just rising. And there they were.

"They sat shimmering in the sky before him. And, as he watched, Shōtoku Taishi called on his courtiers, summoning one of each six ranks, calling them one at a time. He charged each rank of his court to protect two specific parts of the law. As they all assumed this rule, they formed a rainbow that dissolved into the sky.

"Nobuhiro summoned his secretary. He dictated an account of what he had seen and heard in his dream. He then wrote to the most renowned puppet-makers of Awaji, requesting them to create these puppets. When completed, he requested that the most skilled puppeteers from that place come North, and perform his vision before his court and his subjects. In this way, he implanted the seeds of civilization into the soil of the Northern Islands. Afterwards, this was performed whenever a new governor came to rule.

"By Nobuhiro's command, we became the puppet masters responsible for the continuity of this tradition. Our family upheld this obligation until the Meiji Emperor put an end to it. If that had not happened, you would have been a puppeteer."

6)

Slowly, haltingly, his grandfather removed another small sheaf of papers from the box marked TEXT and read aloud. He tilted up the boxes that contained the effigies of Shōtoku Taishi and then each Courtier as he read the description. He did not try to make them move. He simply had them face each other.

Shōtoku Taishi summons courtier - emerald robes to uphold Knowledge. Gives scroll, proclaims: "Knowledge flourishes when decisions are not made by one person alone."
Courtier bows, withdraws. Shōtoku Taishi summons again, proclaims, gives scroll:
"Force peasants to work only when it does not threaten their livelihood."
Bows, withdraws. Courtier bows, withdraws. Shōtoku Taishi summons again, gives scroll, proclaims: "All must subordinate selves to the public well-being." Bows, withdraws. Shōtoku Taishi summons courtier in sapphire. appoints to uphold Justice, gives scroll, proclaims: "Justice prevails when you fulfill the duties of your office. Courtier bows, withdraws. Shōtoku Taishi summons again, gives scroll and proclaims: "Never envy others." Courtier bows, withdraws. Shōtoku Taishi summons again, proclaims: "Do not let local nobles levy taxes for their own benefit." Bows, withdraws.

His grandfather paused and looked at him intently. "Pay attention." He continued slowly, repetitively.

Shōtoku Taishi summons courtier in sky blue robes to uphold Loyalty, gives him the scroll, and proclaims: "Loyalty is sustained keeping faith with those above and below." Courtier bows, withdraws. Shōtoku Taishi summons again, proclaims: "Self-control and tolerance is the foundation of behavior." Courtier bows, withdraws. Shōtoku Taishi summons again, gives scroll, proclaims: "Recognizing virtue and vice is the foundation of loyalty." Bows, withdraws.

The old man now seemed to tire. He pulls himself together and read and moved the puppets more slowly. He wanted the boy to understand.

Shōtoku Taishi summons courtier in scarlet to uphold Decorum, gives scroll, proclaims:

"Decorum is unfailing if punishments and rewards are made the foundation of order. "
Courtier bows, withdraws. Shōtoku Taishi summons again, proclaims and gives scroll: "Attend to your appointed tasks. Do not confuse your duties with those of others." Courtier bows, withdraws. Shōtoku Taishi summons again, gives scroll, proclaims: "Serve the nation by making the schedule of the court, your schedule." Bows, withdraws.

The boy could see that this vague sketch of a performance was important to his grandfather. He did not want to hurt the old man's feelings. He tried to pay careful attention, but he did not understand. He was bored.

Shōtoku Taishi summons courtier in lilac purple to uphold Benevolence, gives scroll, proclaims: "Benevolence flourishes if commands of the ruler are always obeyed." Courtier bows, withdraws. Shōtoku Taishi summons again, gives scroll, proclaims: "Always behave with absolute correctness." Courtier bows, withdraws. Shōtoku Taishi summons, gives scroll, again, gives scroll, proclaims: "Apply the laws impartially and without favor." Bows, withdraws.

The grandfather saw that the boy's mind was drifting. He too was tiring. So, for the last part of the reading, he sped up.

Shōtoku Taishi summons courtier in dark purple robes, appointed to uphold Virtue. He proclaims and gives scroll: "To cultivate harmony is the supreme virtue." Courtier bows, withdraws. Shōtoku Taishi summons again, gives a scroll, proclaims: "The Buddha, the teachings and the community of practitioners are the great support of virtue." Courtier bows, withdraws

That night, the boy had a dream so vivid, he was sure he was living in a different world. He was standing by the door of a gallery at the court of Prince Shōtoku Taishi. He was a guard of some kind and so very attentive. He saw the Prince walk by him on the way to an audience with the entire court.

When he woke up, he was unsure where he was. He tried to go back to the world of the dream but could not.

Occasionally, fragments of that dream returned, but never for more than a second. The boy, and later when he became a man, would wake up trying to capture it but could not.

After a while he forgot it altogether. But he did not forget the afternoon when his grandfather had showed him the puppets.

7.)

He wandered amid the ruins, he thought he could hear someone, maybe his grandfather, sing.

"Under a hard and barren sun,
I stumbled on an unmarked path
Where words lived on
And meanings did not."

40 – ANTHONY PROCOPIO ROSS
USA

ABDUCTION

The tree branches danced in tight packs, arching over the opening of a needle-worked, moonlit forest pathway. A single human figure sunk itself in the dark shadings of the night sky in view of the expanse blossoming into trail, and then, footsteps leapt suddenly onward.

Tracks were left behind crunching woodchips in foggy headspace that allowed them to be left behind the bowed head of an apparition in no real calculable attempt to hide oneself. It knew only how to progress forward and onwards towards the vast, a few forgotten number of moments away.

Grasp lingered no longer than a few instants in the deep wrinkles domed under the walker's skull. Its arrangement lied only in the fulcrum of a non-apparent final destination. Longing lingered tree lines. The path was meant for feet and leaves, where thoughts scattered kaleidoscopically into brush.

The undertaking left mental notes on every fallen twig in plain view, yet sight was shook; hopelessly trudging gaze along like a ghost of the recently deceased. It all felt normal and not far from what can be considered real. A mind could only take so much wandering in a straight line. An unseen horizon called itself forth.

Foliage began to call warnings that felt like wind and sounded of whispering. Cold autumn breeze blanketed the path. This wind felt its way through the woodchips, into the ears, and onto the deaf-awareness of the visitor. It could feel the onset of shivering overtake a torso linked to chill-bumped loose arms hanging at its side.

The wind parted when the body shot off into a sprint. It knew better than to linger and pressed itself, instead, on the outline of the figure as a star draws a tail, into nightfall. Uneven breathes battled headway and gestured to loose gusts from stopping footpath in its tracks.

Movement enabled momentum to find its way: advancing.

This did not stop roots cast from years of growing grossly out of the ground from finding the shadow of an ankle in half step, and tearing it back to the ground in a terrible half-crescent decent: face first, body second, burying velocity with it.

The body laid there, frozen and wondering, while the rest of the world continued to hum in the background. Soon, fingers found themselves clenching palms and chunks of ground, curling the rest of the body awake in a clockwork stuttering machination. Grip laced calves tight enough to cease pain but hard enough cause bruising. Hands pushed hard off of kneecaps and shook with the same haltered push that sustained eyes to continue headfirst.

...

Gentle stepping poked light holes into the earth. One leg drew ceaseless constellations softly behind the first. Landscape flew slower than before.

Gluckstadt Road
for Kingston Frazier

Between the lucky & the ground,
fire squirms in its saddle. A face
is unable to fly unless it is
destroyed. The stolen long
for the highway like a flower
lapping up a whisper. A child
is a city at the center of amber,

can't eat *according to*. The difference
is glazed in change, a red
that searches the breath. Being
is a borrowed dog chewing dice.
a pink calamity under
the bed. Order can double a blight,
the whole groan. What is anything
unkind but a number scattering

the red gate? We climb a large box,
& sometimes the sound makes us
three. To be light is to be left
open, wings silver & trembling
a church. Many particles suppose
a slender machine, serene & dark
& stretched into aloha. A widow

is a shadow rearranging the house,
but the best use of grace
is cupping the head, feeding
a joint to red water, sickening
a crystal. A feather is leaning in
the water. Lean into the wind.
Show that leaning needs little.
Jam a feather in the sound.

42 - ERIC PIERZCHALA
USA

A Portrait of Aunt Mina (Framed by Our Last Conversation, Enlivened by the Objects in Her House, Clarified by Events Therein)

"Many died in 1919, many tombstones prove it," but it's
the saints illuminated in her fairly-done attempts to copy
the old master's paintings who stand out from the crowd
even as they head off to market to buy day-old fish and
hard-skinned pomegranates, though the saints, they look

naked, exposed; perhaps because they've forgotten their halos
back at home. Stiff, the constraint of Elizabethan ruffled courtesan collars
chokes the cheeks out of a rose-colored peach into a state of still
life, and while one boy sees Thor's hammer in Bryce's Canyon
another simultaneously sees one on a U.S. marine's tombstone.

In another corner of the globe, seeing where a cocky rooster was
headed, the old sly fox wishes he could head it off, but not being
a murderer at heart, or, liking especially the sight of blood—riddle
it to death. But it's like seeing in the dark as the distance of the uncrossed
distance becomes clearer to the eye, as the mind focuses

in upon it; gathers in more light, and makes the shapes
of the off yonder, there, more defined and disappear
to a vanishing point, where, the point all along was proximity
and always has been—to where, it all seems to point to a point—
to a metal arrow which directs our attention to the blue glow

of a box where upon the screen a mime in whiteface draws up
a sketch of comic patter about being perplexed by the consistency
of pancake batter as it was all once separately: buttermilk, salt,
and flour, and as the plumped-up politician stands upon his stump
speech and claims that every fourth line would have a rhyme

in time, we waited, and waited, guided by his anaphora,
as overhead in the searchlights the buxom curves of bombs
and experimental B-42s fall from the sky, together,
whistle and buzz, as a matchbook colored apple, white,
and blue, with a red "V" emblazoned upon the cover for

the expected victory—ignites—in the jade-green ashtray
and in a blaze burns a world and map to ash. And now
grandfather's pocket watch in the desk drawer starts ticking
off the time, chimes at the half hour "it's the seconds that
never fly backward enough," and on the quarter hour

"regret is not a word to be trifled, but with, no with." Meanwhile,
the radioman says the third "little Mozart" has been discovered
this month, this one, he says, also uses too many notes—
then adds, that the road paved in yellow brick was found
to lead to a dead end, but he asks: is it not that the best,

worst, and all in between have been created and shaped by
violent collisions—while the cat looks out the window disconcerted by
the coexistence of light and oncoming shadow, and the dog barks
at a whistle no human ear could hear, and feeling the hot, heavy air press
down upon me I'm awakened by hearing Aunt Mina say:

"I was first married, twice..." but, as both history local-familial and
worldwide has shown, ambiguity is as democratic to the "T" as
any model which can produce just enough to live, and survive on,
and also get a bite to eat, or, even get you from A to B, so,
I never ask her to explain, further, nor ask for another dry scone.

The Ranch Was Ever in the State of Meanwhile

An otherwise useless building, asbestos, mold, be damned and we will, is filled up with: pieces, anything an artist, he, she, she has made—dreamed, seemed—and could carry up the stairs and could beg to call, "art," standard low, high, whatever you may, and you may: invite the people, the old, the young, who legally can drive and drink to the worst part of the city one can think, where they will come for the night of "culture" which is promised to thrive within a dilapidated building, a known modern dive, but then they, just may, even and again, might all be fooled like a lost 16th century and call the whole thing a renewal—a god forbid Renaissance, as in, the deep dark shadows of the music hall, a mouse sits eating a quick dry crumb enjoying the soulful silence of the dusty mood, lazy, loose, as he stands upright upon sharp carpet, soon, to scurry-on-off in a moment's time, notice, warning, noise...but for now he stays, still, safe within loud silence to his sensitive sentient ears, as a lonely man, tan, gone gray, returns from his day of long toil and thinks to himself: what an empty life that some, may lead, and they will, be damned, that maybe he has led...as he: looks for a morsel in his cupboard, bare, to make a dirty dish, a plate which to clean or to make his life mean, all, something. As he stops, and picks up a pencil, but then chooses instead a blue pen, and begins to trace his lonely name and make a print of his hand, a self-portrait of face, with no hidden shame, a blue fingerprint, left, and he wonders if of his name he could somehow sell, and begs the question, well, what shall we eat?

43 – DALE MICHAEL HOUSTMAN
USA

Selected Segadas from "The Rose-Jacket Almanacs of the Louche Monk"

19
Snow on a faded red curtain recalls to me a failing industry in a country's interior.

24
The secret history of the Sentimental is an umbrella in the rubble.

27
Tradition does not tamper but it is touched. Habit is that insanity made as a cure for chaos.

44
Today, and quite by accident, I discovered that no mechanism – no matter how finely engineered – will turn a wolf into a nightingale

.60
How anxious some citizens will always be to flaunt their modesty, a false perfection that is mostly unearned.

85
Even the laziest chicken doesn't have the time to be frisked.

88
The logic of the trout will never pay all the debts of the river.

97
Toss a stone at a poet's head to elicit a mild fluorescence. My favorite flashlight.

103

Sleep is a dissident colony which I travel across to strike up a shallow conversation with the man in front of me.

113
There is even a darkness which stinks of opinion.

116
There exists a certain type of luxury even in poverty, but no trainstations.

117
Injured anarchists should strive to own sleds.

119
What is most obscure? A sophisticated joy.

123
When we settle for ourselves, we flatten out, and may thus be delivered under the door.

127
I am a faded humanist, a river of half-smoked cigarettes.

132
A limpid green bird in a turtle's nest. Please have it arranged for me.

141
Why do the citizens sleep? Most have no consciousness to refresh, and their wakefulness is a thin blanket.

146
Pale women inspire florid poetry.

158
Big speeches fill little graveyards.

167
An orange is that dress which a symphony imagines wearing.

169
The Sun disdains human virtue and only desires the homage of blindness.

170

Obscurity is the little sister of oblivion, so you're bound to end up with two sisters.

189

This century's dirt is disturbingly comforting.

190

It appears that existence gets in the way of your own best interests.

241

Beliefs are cheap souvenirs from an expensive holiday.

268

You can devour any door simply by opening it.

281

Strangeness is a labor-intensive delight, so I am never unemployed, only unpaid.

321

Bamboo is just a ghost yawning.

333

The church piano, an exhausted coral elephant.

342

Any ladder looks sincere leaning against a drowned hospital.

354

Reading a good book, and immediately forgetting it forms one of my sharpest pleasures.

401

Only yesterday I watched a train, the distant blue snow, and a fish. My heart was not in the audience.

433

I have noticed that some self-liberated persons construct tombs in which doorbells have been installed, because they not only wish to ignore visitors, but also to let them know they are being ignored.

490

The overused word "pretty" is like a government dossier upon the fog.

513

Rain will not readily agree to be a passenger.

529

Friendship is an apron constructed from a single rotten acorn.

592

Like potholes on the Spice Road, distance only earns second-rate applause.

620

The Ridiculous chokes upon that substance which the Absurd abstains from.

633

I often wonder if the graves and the clarinets have put aside all their differences.

658

*Stars seem an indifferent courtesy,
and recall to my mind a field of treacherous horses.*

661

Although the wind is the natural groom of the candle's flame, it must always look forward to being a widower.

662

It is strange that not many people make hats out of candles.

947

A book is a Roman fireside after the empire has been extinguished.

After the Simple Wars

After the Simple Wars, many splendid funeral feasts were held, some lasting an entire week, which was very pleasing to Queen Perforation, whose efficient vanity and devout love of degenerate luxury was known to all her subjects, and publicly applauded, so as to avoid extermination. She owned five platinum carriages, a "poverty holiday" walkup in the quaint village of Stane-on-Westcutt, and hundreds of little service boys dressed up as soldiers, who were fated to die in the next series of wars she loved to have with neighboring countries, who had never done anything to her but ruin her view of the sea with their church spires and castles, which was not very aggressive of them when one thinks about it. But let's not. But Queen Perforation enjoyed dreaming of the slaughter, and so many of her people suffered because —well — because. Such things will happen, and is it not our duty to bear pain and daily humiliation with a smile? Many of us think so. Or think we must think so.

King Perforation XIII was meanwhile hanging by his ankles in the main root cellar, for he was a perturbation to the Queen, who had always believed that he should be grandiose and opulent rather than merely benevolent. But even the adorable daydreams about his suffering had begun to bore her, so she sent word all through her kingdom of her desire to attend some diverting entertainment that didn't involve the King's humiliating position. So several of her more loyal followers hurried into their wagons, and set out to find some amusements for their Queen. In short time, they had discovered three dogs who could whistle operettas through their fingers, and a huge copper statue of a nose, and a few odd slivers of something the local townsfolk claimed were once parts of a magic mill-house that could turn petty thieves (or just passing strangers) into a nutritious flour, from which they made People Cakes. The scarpering loyalists hoped (even beyond the question of the Queen's being difficult to distract from hangings and decapitations) that this last item at least would stop their ruler from having them hanged, for they were selfish, and valued their small existences. and so it goes with such delicate solipsists. We who are brave in the face of our degradation revile them!

Yet the dogs failed to whistle on command and were gutted with a rusty brooch – which made it much more unlikely that they would perform magnanimously in the future. The copper nose began to run and repulsed the Queen, and was quickly melted down for pots and pans. Worst of all, the broken shards turned out to be merely the remnants of a alehouse drain pipe. Her Insufferable Highness was both mortified and (as expected) furious, and so ordered the would-be entertainment-providers to be hung up next to the King, who rather relished the thought of company, to the point that his eyes grew as large as serving platters, although they remained empty of any nourishment for the Queen. For this impertinence, his most precious spouse had him beaten with a newly forged copper pot, and (for good measure) tossed the entire royal council into the sea, although she could not see this because of all the intervening church spires and castles. Several thousand people watched this display of temper, and found it rather common, and intensely ho-hum. Such things will happen, and is it not our pleasure to be crushed beneath barrels of pickles with a heart full of Germanic lieder? Many of us think so. Or think we must think so.

Next a soldier (named Fetcher Juggle) stepped forth and boasted to the Queen that he would ride out into the greater world, returning with a marvel that would stagger even her Blessed Gratuitousness. He tied an opportunity ladder upon his nag, Yokel's Heart, and rode away to the dismal fanfare of a single bent trumpet, for all the other heralds had been burnt at the stake for wrong notes. But the intrepid cavalier was — in fact — merely a shoemaker, and he was only putting his best foot forward in his very best shoes, hoping to gain a little favorable traction in the eyes of his Overripe Ruler. It was a big mistake, but a well-intended one, which is not to be sniffed at in an age of ill-intended mistakes.

Oh, how dark and disagreeable were the inns that Fetcher Juggle passed by, with alarm drums beating in the hot air, and phalanxes of marching feet hidden off behind the hedgerows, and all the women wearing greasy leather aprons and shoddy slippers as they leant in their shadowed doorways, decrepit mothers standing where only crispy fresh daughters stood a short time back. Once, he looked through the iron grating of a stone prison and saw two pigs struggling inside a bag until pair of magic jade scissors refashioned them into a petite corset. "So that is how corsets are born, and what a diverting surprise!" he thought to himself. Still, he felt that even this would not be amusement enough for his Dark Gloriosity, who had once seen a square of night-colored silk re-cut into a villager's wife. "So that is how wives are born, and what a diverting surprise!" she had thought to herself, and promptly fallen into a boredom deeper than before. Many people died that night. Another common sight.

And so he rode on, passing doors marked with chalk scribblings of tiny birds in unique postures. The shoemaker longed for a door unmarked with a tiny bird, and then he went to sleep while his horse carried him deep into the Kissoff Forest, where there were no doors and thus no chalk birds upon doors. "This is as close to Heaven as many of us are likely to get," the shoemaker thought. Such things will happen, and is it not our fate to be pushed down a dark hole with a giggle in our throats? Many of us think so.

In the morning, Fetcher's faithful horse had disappeared, and the shoemaker's eyes were as big as copper pots (or pans), for he thought this very strange, and so on. Thus he walked all day through the forest, and then it was midnight, so he took out his tin teacup and sat down on a wet hillside to enjoy himself, for his life had been a very laborious one up until then, and he needed a little rest. Just before he fell asleep, a large eagle appeared before him, and asked him where his horse had gotten to. The shoemaker answered that he felt it must have been stolen, for he had tied it tightly to a small tower from which an odorous liquid seeped. The large bird thought it very likely, and then struck a light to better see the shoemaker's face, for he was a curious beast, although quite beautiful after the foreign fashion.

After staring at the shoemaker, (who was quite ugly after the foreign fashion) the bird opened his cavernous craw, and spewed out a set of fine (if somewhat thickly moist) clothes which he told the shoemaker to put on. When he had done this, the eagle instructed him to get on his back, and he would take him to an elegant room up in the clouds where he would also be reunited with his mount, Yokels Heart. The shoemaker was dismayed to discover that this was a lie, for the eagle carried him high into the mountains and tied him to a lone tree in the center of a barren rock field, where he left him to bemoan a wasted life and a bad ending, and such a such. Each night, sparks flew down from the leaves above his head and set fire to his fine (and now completely dry) set of clothes, until he was quite naked. Thus is vanity a fleeting thing. And every morning, the shoemaker (being somewhat talented and resourceful) sewed together a new set of clothes from the leaves above his head, until he looked like a forest elf. Thus did many months go by.

One night (just before the sparks were about to start raining down on him) a yellow witch appeared and gave Fetcher Juggle a tinder-box, saying "I am now your only true friend. Strike this tinder-box with your needle, and you will be set free." So he did, and a huge obsidian stairway appeared in the distance, up which he ran, anxious to escape imprisonment, even if he was only to run into a different set of dangers. At the top, he found himself standing in a garden, and decided it would be a relaxation to attend the garden theatre, which was showing a play entitled "A Little Money Goes Nowhere" which bored him greatly. However, the role of the Pleasant Gentleman was played by the very eagle who had kidnapped him, so he schemed to avenge himself upon his persecutor. He made his way to the backstage door and waited there with a well-made boot in his hand. Everybody knows you shouldn't cross a shoemaker. Well, many of us think so. His own boots were now mending themselves in a garret and all for the price of only two shillings, which bankrupted the poor villagers for miles around. Many of his friends had once had fine clothes, but none had owned a pair of fine boots.

Meantime, the Pendant King was having a fine old time imagining that he was seated in an ostentatious hippodrome by the side of a river that flowed from the highest window of a castle, in which his once beautiful daughter was cleaning his boots with a tinderbox made from a melted trumpet. While he was thus dreaming of a wonderful night of horse racing distraction, a yellow witch appeared in his cell and cut off his head with a golden pocket watch after whipping him for several years with a rocking-horse tail. Gold coins fell from his open eyes. "Good morning!" said the yellow witch and turned into the Repugnant Queen, who now had wheels that were tiny heads attached to her heels. Realizing that her Easygoing spouse was now a part of the "greater company", she threw away the golden coins, and kept the rocking-horse tail for remembrance. Then she closed his eyes with a happy chortle, and put on a greasy leather apron, so she could walk among the villagers without seeming too splendid. It worked, for she was never splendid again. Teacups and a hundred lamps were growing from a tree.

"Not a truly horrible tale," thought Fetcher Juggle, but just then the large eagle reappeared and took him off to a tea party in the hollow of a tree which grew from the Thundering Queen's forehead. He had been to the wars, and now he was returning home.

All this amused the Queen greatly, and she repaid him with a small chalk bird.

fenestra!

moaners of the Pandaria Tangent!
now is the time to cry
the big circular fenestra! fenestra!
(system voice Vicki) and even be a ligament

the orgy to reduce hassle
begins with the six morals of the yogi
a talk for the poly-deviant

we've launched a camel from the delicate bamboo
the Q&A touched on everything
finalists provided by the Crochet Redeemer Bursar
will disarm the enormity for our postmaster of the cannabis
these poly-deviants also shake
cocaine, crank cocaine, effectiveness and heroin
or other escapist tendencies then orgy to reduce hassle
again
where surplus is a problem
producing or cultivating or supplying
to the englishman of July

because one pestilence is small small
go be small
it is a sad figment all we have is each other
I knew something was wrong, fenestra
then I heard muttering something wonderful
someone just sits down and plays a piano
into the open field of existence

the word we use in English is multitudes
YOU KNOW I'M RIGHT
bring me your most romantic chickens and frogs
just stop and imagine how a chimera feels
just for awhile do that

it's starting to matter who you are

and it feels wonderful
like a parlor muzzle
the pleasure of making a room
for others to lie down in mystery
sleep here
the music is all on my face
like one of my girdles

my device
talks to or about the new luminary
can you imagine
wonderful fences
all over and perfect
my grammar dropping bonnets on them
in the cardigan
in the drug
talking about the new lump

people are having the most wonderful feelings
bonus on them
some kind of fenestra presence
in the beer too
one realizes one
is one about to eat one's own face
a face that is something from a book not just any book
"help finally arrived"
when it came for me
I almost ate my button
in a cold and lonely field
I assure you
it is both an opening in this house
and an opening in the ear

a bird just flew in my fenestra.
sat down and played the piano too

the portal—shout into it sing into it
pretend we're making room for some traveler
you there me here

and the underpass biographer has died
he always said he was good-looking
a stream sang his 'long black veil' in fury

and the fenestra has gone invisible
you can only see it
on a wish at dusk in the filament
and say we don't have much but
where a steamer sirloins for us

Where we were going

It is a great fear of mine that one day I will
be physically incapable of asking questions.

Sometimes in dreams I can't,
and in one I followed a crowd
before wondering
(but not asking because I couldn't)
where we were going.

Of course,
I couldn't ask, so I fell behind,
wandering alone,
but desperately wanting to catch up with the group.

I listened for their voices
and came upon a fountain
walled with brick and stone.

As I peered into the clear blue water
I found terra cotta hibiscuses
Floating in the stead of lilies.
Man made and abundant,
Yet radiantly beautiful things

Everyone created without explanation or apology
But I wanted to know
How could they float?

My Dear Louise

I love you in red.
Love your bloody
brilliant little babe
trapped
in big red balloon
of birth and legs
of petals all pink --
girl-gore, waterborne
platelets. Wait.

Did you ever see her
show? Dinner party.
Salads on platelets.
I laugh. Such a great
chilly day in Chicago.
It was all the rage.
I was a nymphlet
myself at the time
and the view made me
red with wonder.
She refrained from
the menacing menses
but not you, my love
not you. Why I love you
best for absofucking sure.

So back to us,
my dearest dear
Louise. I love you
r blackness, spiders
ink spots, holes.
You did black up
right.

And the creams.

Simple cottons,
cradles and breasts
and scrotums and
stuffed dolls and pricks,
which reminds me.

Once I wrote a poem
about the Large
Glass, one her and
nine hims (were they
suitors or thieves?)
Even with him I was
most struck with you
connected and separate
as we all must be
taking turns as brides
taking turns as bachelors
taking turns at the bullshit,
the dividing line between.

But I love you
most when you cringe
(not one of 'them')
so how could I help
but mention him?
Don't be mad at me.
Let's both just
give him bloody
hell and then see if
Teeny can come out
to play. (Some will think
that naughty but it ain't
. . . well it is now . . .
always was maybe and
something else too.)

For I love you
dearest Louise
from the bottom
of my feet
unseen
unravelling
as red as your hand

across a dancing page.
I love you in red,
although you always
preferred blue. I laugh.
The contradictions
allure, holy shititude.
So always, almost mine.
So most assuredly you.

100 Years of Love

In the beginning was the story
of a top hat and a cigar,
and thorns that tightened about them
while they blew kisses at the ocean.
There were prayers along the clifftops,
weddings at which strong men whistled
and the gathered wildflowers became birds.
Transvestite ballerinas duelled with sticks
and breakfast was always served,
promptly at 7, among the hayricks.
After the honeymoon, the forest grew deeper
and its leaves could turn as a caress
or grasp the wrists of the faithless.
The women who came leaping from its heart
wore smiles and love letters,
and had no fear of flying machines.
Instead of weeping, their business
was a black feather and the loom's beat.
"Cut off your hair", cried the signalman,
"and feed it to the keyhole".
So they did, supple witches with cameras,
directing the fall of meadowlarks.
"Sit and wait", said the manager,
so they did, and the armour grew on them
until they were glass, and shadow, and lace,
mysterious as locked doors,
and the fur of them crept like smoke
or chloroform. No taxis could be found.
Weddings were as veiled as funerals.
The knife was always concealed as a kiss.
Young couples were butchered by the mob.
Only on beaches was there any respite,
where old men dived like gulls at beauty queens.
And men were poison, the headlamps of their eyes
raping the cobbled streets into ruins.
The sound of gunfire was heard

in the factories and in the barracks,
the night sky lit up like broken windows,
men walked with their backs bent.
So philosophers wondered, what is this love?
The children might have answered,
wreathed as they were in futures,
but they were too quick for philosophy.
In the last years of the century, love failed.
Everyone left on trains to distant places.
Nobody was waiting at the station when they arrived.
Gossip lingered on doorsteps for a day,
fed the pigeons, scrubbed the pavement,
and walked away at last, smoking a pipe.

Correspondence with Ithell

Our letters were all that the board of Bishops
would allow. Savage and mundane, written
on pebbles or bark, they ran like aurochs
in heat; and flocks of postmen greeted
each one by adding a new carytid
to the palace of lupine dreams. Our script
was ogham, our voices the whisper of leaves.
How beautiful it was, that dialogue
between the star and the wave, and even now
it murmurs deep within the holy thicket
in tongues of intelligent lust.
In those days, we lived in the bliss of the damned,
the moon's phases were ours, as were the dusk
and the starlings' murmurations.
We would read books like auguries,
in libraries of bronze and lapis lazuli.
Our children have forgotten the wonders of the age,
becoming less than we were, as they shrink
like rotten mushrooms. We had our rage,
our passions, and they overflowed the sea.
Where the green sea meets the grey sky,
where the points of the compass rose meet,
that was our collective destination;
the journey immanent in our alphabets.
The correspondences broke out
from lettered cages, the academies fell
one after another like volumes
of the magical dictionary. Then
it was over, sudden as the death of horses
and as frothing, wild-eyed.
We accumulated dust and years.
Now, my letters are as full of meaning
as they are meaningless, and recycled
from drums and the doom of cattle.
I miss the cadences of stone and leaf,
while archivists pick over the bones
of old correspondence with their knives and forks,
and the dog-eared works of biography
gather as monumental as the geese
readying themselves for migration.
She and I are a memory,

consequent as patterns in nature.
While, here's the nub, our correspondences
still take flight in the dark shadowed woodlands
of the heart. Our letters are unbound
and freed, in their invisibility
and in their indivisibility,
to penetrate where others will not,
where they accumulate, as demons must.

48 - YOSHE MALKUS
Germany

Under the Sea is a Ship on Fire

In a mind isolated to this reality through delusive senses.

Ed Edward or Edward Ed was completely disassociated from reality with quite violent attitudes and a described complex psychology due to extensive expedition of dimensions and fighting in war for nine years unavoidably exposed to great aggression, hallucinating enormously – sleep walking through an isolated world – his mind. Sometimes he would get glimpses of the norm but what did it matter, not able to distinguish, not even being aware that something was different with his. He often shunned public - a necessity to maintain balance – on remote black shore we find examples of artists to be between being and into greater areas of the construct of conflict for nearly any given subject or matter - free as a captured mole dependent on the verbal world otherwise anonymous. Seeming normal from the outside from the inside.

Somehow under the sea is a ship on fire.

He arrived at home 'The Valley of Death' - made for exhibition purposes – avoided the four hundred all together clustered dead, turned directly onto a bottle of vodka, filled a glass and took a shot. Others were brutally wounded and suffered enormously – particularly artists. Occasionally he found bodies had been moved, scenarios had been created, scenes were staged. Depictions of acts of murder, torture, of the mutilation with the richness of implication in character and aesthetic sense. The artist aroused used his fullest potential - odd fascination for crime in this early work. Harmlessness – that simply does not exist after all.

Some recreations were even staged years later. This development has totally the tendency to create, to become chaos.

However, the newspaper reporting of harsh conditions elsewhere. Countries sought for expansion of power against their enemy - he foreshadowed world war in near time.

Rest in peace.

Smoke from cigarettes fuming in the air creating an impenetrable cloud soon filling the whole room not being able to see his own hands. Who lit the butts in the ashtray again, he had no pets he believed. Red glowing little grinning faces watching him, laughing at him, making fun of him through the haze trying to figure out how to take off his head while cutting a handful frozen fingers into pieces having no idea what else better to do – the only food he had found laying around (they were in the fridge) except for his stuffed armadillo so that doesn't count. Sometimes the feel overcame him a ghost was living within when objects were moved or vanished completely. Thief! A combination of stuffed armadillo and supernatural mist as roommate that never pays the rent. He threw it out of the window which shattered into thousands of pieces on the street. The smoke got unbearable filling every bit of Ed's body, inside of his organs – he decided to jump out a window also. More splintering glass.

Blood as red as red wine or ketchup in veins and vampire gets drunk sucking this rather inhuman human being or someone else does.

Ed went out to a restaurant because his inner stomach had told him he was hungry. Never had he learned the weird language of hunger that growls like a tiger jabbed in the ass, immediately the neural transmitters are instinctive not shooting the information into the head but with immense speed right through it creating a hole like a gunshot through which all inside leaks upside down towards the nebulas of where the trapped, now free spirit belongs to – came from – a defends mechanism reflex making possible for the living not to suffer and the dead not to live like a chicken whose head has been chopped off but still running around searching and picking for grains with a phantom head not realising it's dead. Immune to the rising pain for those few seconds the beast is left looking confused around. Inappropriate aggressive useless fucks. As if the situation couldn't have been solved by talking with each other like the civilized persons they were. It always had to come down to murder or violence. Would rot in hell for that – or at least in jail. Somehow Ed had a pretty good feeling since he remembers for what it was saying – inherent until birth (again).

When going while in deep thoughts, travelling inside, when swimming and forgetting the water, blind for the outside looking, watching thoughts streaming, trance, afterwards it's like a physical blackout, different perception of time in your mind, tricked into teleportation by destroying imaginary ticking clocks that keep away from knowing what is important for the human to feel – the moment. What happens in the future and the past, memory and anxiety, you don't eat, drink, fuck in the future neither in the past, may have but not anymore, just now. Being, no going to be no have been. You are not thinking tomorrow or yesterday, times is an illusion that keeps off, wasting what you have 'til you don't have it, getting high on oxygen pumping through veins, fill lungs as if they were birthday balloons, if that would happen some other time than this immediate particle of now, in a week maybe two getting the money, you would asphyxiate very soon, so why let everything else you think you value let happen when it doesn't exist for now. There is no such thing as future when trying to be futuristic but future is now so being now is being the future. Getting so obsessed with the act of shooting that the target becomes invisible and missing it. Today tomorrow of yesterday. Wait!

Arriving somewhere where the restaurant should have been nothing familiar was recognized so he walked backwards back until he stood in front of where he wanted to stand in front of – a small shabby place where all kinds of people hung around – drunks, artists, psychopaths, addicts, and so on, – no community he would very likely fit in. Mostly not more than one or two were to be seen at once, but it was cheap and he liked to read the uninteresting articles out of the free magazines that were scattered all over the place – they were never the same ones what kept it interesting.

He ordered a headache with tinnitus.

The brain is screaming like a dehydrated flamingo coloured whale in a lake of hot yellow white egg soup giving birth to a chimpanzee - a quite humanlike creature, or rather the other way around - feet first, three times, three lives and a miscarried fetus, another one though not really. A soulless wrinkled blood-sodden pack of soft rubber like pink skin overdrawn bones with typical Hollywood movie alien proportions – no one knew if the tragedy had a physical cause and how long the fetus had been this way – guesses were made seemingly, truth was, there wasn't thinking going on in the doctors brain, he just babbled unununderstandable nonsense not to understand, actually there wasn't any conscious brain activity going on behind the cell shell of what is called a skull, insignificant – no one cared because there was no one to do so, with the ability to. Maybe some memory flash overcame the half developed in a constant dream state being creature which lead to a shock which caused death of mind because it wasn't evolved enough to handle a trauma caused by reality of a long forgotten time - today.

When he was in Korea in that one restaurant with some friends he freshly met outside, he didn't understand no word they spoke because he couldn't speak the Korean tongue and they weren't talking to him. Calling them friends in his head. Brought was a bowl arranged in front of him. Tentacle arms taking hold of him – slimy and wet ink tinctured space cadet blueberry colored. Losing unconsciousness while remaining conscious is final DEATH. Dissolving of the soul. Luckily Edward just lost consciousness fading into black; void.

Writing as escapism.

Lighting soundless and roaring thunder, clattering waterfall from the sky. Heavy rain from the high in the sky dark shadowed clouds. For a while, then silence. Again.

Female fish spatting their soft spawn in blue lagoon deserts on a grey day – bad weather. Still. Small translucent balls rolling with long shady tails, made by the huge burning evening fireball roughly about 9 multiplied by 10 million miles away, disguised as tumbleweed not identified as interesting by the hunting observing organs of possible enemies but also lacking any attention and affection by the tricked of their own far developed gene product protection technics by nature but low intelligent parents permanently chewing moist snuff and drinking a mixture of sprinkling water and diaphanous wine, widely known as wine spritzer which is a beverage alcoholics failing to get off addiction would choose to lie progress to themselves and others in their never-ending battle. Also their husbands unable to recognise concluding into non fertilization of their forever restless wandering lost not existing predestined children. Many offspring without father – few without mother. Some with no one at all. A bunch without themselves.

Strange visions were troubling Ed at night when sleeping/believing to sleep – unusual contradictions to his so ordinary day to day live. At least always forgetting the events of recent body and mind resting periods. Sometimes he confounds things and didn't know if it really happened or if it happened during being asleep. Doesn't make a big difference was concluded.

Bowling shoes! He wanted to buy bowling shoes goddamn.

Recurring flashbacks plaguing him for months now. Unpleasant déjà-vus – glimpses, a gate into a parallel universe, taking the longest seconds ever experienced. There are few possibilities what is happening exactly when the enormous coincidence of parallel universes overlapping eventuates. For this being able to happen the two situations must be for this little amount of time completely, let me repeat that, completely identical. Your being, especially your mind is fusing with your parallel you. You then foresee what will happen in the parallel world or have already lived it in the very past. Also it could be that some accident created this parallel world and the knowing is only an echo of what is happening in the new one from the momentum until both are split separated. A trained traveller will know exactly when he enters and leaves this moment, a layman won't perceive it as such and will just be a little confused until forgotten immediately as another pettiness. People even disappeared in front of eyes of others being absorbed thanks to some mistake in the parallels. Surely they didn't notice a thing leaving sad family members behind whom they still had, but nobody is to blame... except for the lord almighty god himself. But nobody is to blame.

There is no scientific explanation of course like for all not physical things and mathematics is made up by people, too – everything is based on algorithms, or are algorithms based on everything, rather? An abstraction – non-existent. Kind of like language is – a tool for simple communication, yes, preventing us to use all our intellect. Our way of thinking is caged in the possibilities that words give us because it is rooted so deep down and we're in an age where we explored all there is with this option and improvement wouldn't do and diction is evolving backwards anyways with the stultification of members of consuming society and laziness, especially in challenging of brain and the will to think for oneself and create new. The inside cannot be seen anyway, just how things seem is important, or can it? By like-minded or people with rudiments. And is not that a greater pleasure? – there is more though.   But words are not enough.

Masturbation marathon, singing saws, drilling claws like clinging laws.

Where were we is where we are. Ed was where no man's car could go. Lands far beyond the human forms, no importance has any large number of golden coins.

A coffee is what he needed now. Another coffee simultaneously. Terrible poor orange juice gin long drinks he was sick of by now the bar was providing, their smell already sticking to last century suit pants while dripping wet cigarettes nicotine desperate attempts to be resorbed failed most pathetic in ripped open papers.

Cogitations streams drifting unobtrusively from topic to topic, from sentence to sentence, from word to word, to content nothingness.

Insect windows from the other side staring full emptiness throughout tarmac television screen noises stretching airplane nozzle sounds support motorcycle engines. Growing house facades squinting over to tables poisoning liquids, ambivalent calming effect and cooling the flowing blood appearing as dwindled veins. Shitting blood. Centipede ear worm scrabbling, then stuck in bitter cerumen initiating its production leading to a bothersome tickling inside one of those holes in your head. Six to let the light shine through.

Creativity flows like oil did in the Gulf of Mexico. Overthrown coffee mug, stains. Deepwater Horizon Oil Spill.

Rudely Awakened.

A full length on the back lying figure – paralysed in bed with blanket all the way up to bristly chin watching different sized blurred silhouettes. The room full of spiders scribbling everywhere while his gaze followed the creatures on the still letting dim gloaming from the blue hour nightfall in curtains up to the ceiling where the bigger critters hiding in corners. It was good having some company. A good diversion to otherwise isolated days. Yes, it was dextromethorphan. You can buy dxm in every pharmacy completely legal without prescription when asking for the cough medicine it is in. But you'll need a lot of it. Doesn't pay. Rather go for codeine.

Other times sleep paralysis. Didn't scare him, waking up not able to move. He enjoyed miscellaneous experiences of this body- and mind-altering circumstances with fascination absorbing as much of it as possible. Also suicide attempts, was a chronic part of his life for the kicks. For the feeling of coming home in cold winter to sit in thy arm chair on the Persian carpet in front of crackling fire with some warm drink and cigar maybe reading, for the greatest relief. Especially the first and grand finale. Believe me and give it a try to go back where you come from, - whatever your religions synonym is for the nodimensional all surrounding all-pervasive untouchable timeless pneuma/ rûaḥ (רוּחַ.) Is it god, nirvana, tau, nothing or void when you're a nihilist, the flying spaghetti monster or vegetables etc. We, the living were sent to walk in a world of dead form, might call it hell. (Parts of the) cosmic consciousness forming the few zillion organisms, when dying becoming part of the whole again, when created a part split of it. But not really because it's everywhere anyway. The brain is the mysterious connection and transmitter of physical to pneuma and receiver of pneuma to physical. Humans are relatively high developed so they're conscious about both but the brain is constructed in a way so we're bound to ours with those memories and thought patterns our body grasped as long as the impulses are balanced how they're intended to be. Who we are is a combination of brain and mind. Your construct of brain and body determines your form of mind which is a reaction to your architecture which can change and when it does you may think 'you' have changed. Meditation or psychedelic drugs can bypass this border to an extent and can let you have contact to the 'supernatural'. It's chaos - the contrary to the dead physical world – order. Life as we know it is the dialogue between those. Without one of them the other wouldn't be existent and so wouldn't be the whole. (The universe functions like the brain for the universal consciousness.)

Didn't bother telling.

Outside for a walk here and there little ant men moving nervous and irresolute along the clearly with straight roads connected stars of the wide heaven's tent. Ed was walking in the middle of the street. He hoped to get run over by a car. Caravans of crucified innocents, driven herds by pig priests pelted with dirt until coated mud men on both sidewalks going in different directions in the same. Wherever they go, they will arrive somewhere. Whatever they know, they will arrive nowhere. To be heard are bells of all kinds in the waves of the heights like winds from deep waters. Doorbells, chimes, cowbells, Christmas tones knolled in bedlam fashion by gangs of dwarfs and deformed announcing stimulus satiation. The sign to get the fuck out before it's after too late.

The old whole in the wall circus with red walls was another land of its own and was living a (w)hole lot up to its name. One would immediately find one overwhelmed by nasty slurping, champing and slobbering occupied ambient, neon bulbs, slimy phosphor padded sopping balls and shiny smudgy sperm lipstick while the acts predominantly hidden by sporadically qualitative expensive carnival revetted servants and attendants equivalent to the scene and place. It was glorious. No guarantee this was even a place or real, but when one was there. A naked classy hole in the wall of insanity with carnival frenzy and boy in buttons apes serving free drinks and pills, blotter – as tincture as well, powders of unknown nature and girls, boys, trannies/she-males buckshee. He never knew when, how or where he got out or what, where, how, with whom he did. One thing was for sure as he was taking a bus somewhere else – peeing old sluts is what the captain called his passengers, preferring longingly home after they sucked up his car, drank all the gasoline, emptied the tanks, didn't know if just hours or days passed. Pockets empty to dust, belongings gone, his rumpled hat, cheap perforated coat, a worn off shoe once in a while when he was lucky his head and dick (was still there?). Heard a story about macho man's cock bitten off while deep throating. 'Laughter'. Only worth mentioning danger was catching an artist to share lust and pleasure with. Their tongues and genitals replaced by Cymothoa Exygua. The parasite then feeds from what one gets fed. It becomes one's only chance to articulate outside from the inner expression. A voice in traditional sense, parasite still. Without, the true pure artist wouldn't be able to talk ordinarily or socialise like a - from societies point of view - considered healthy human being. It's sucking one's words and speaks instead for one. Only way to communicate oneself then is to create, find another medium to do so. Modern language is an irritating component to the truth anyways. Help. When diseased by this fellow doesn't make you an artist, you maybe just had sexual contact/ intercourse with one or another diseased who got stricken by it from elsewhere, for example from making out or further more with a fish. In very exceptional cases patients had an 'asshole's tongue'.

Glitter curtains, blurred distortions.

- looks cool though. Nostalgic reminder of the puppet horror movies used puppets.

Dodgy guise carries backdoors (if thus was) dead cat in a bag to the trash startling more cause turmoil around heaps of nibbled garbage bag rotten zombie cat stacks, their cannibal feast violated by the arrival of more offering. Inside the club cats sniffing glue without clue. The 'Glue sniffin' cat's blues' playing. Then the 'Dead cat in a bag's jazz'. A tiny along driving past behind the scenes look into unknown underground scenes evoke yearning to get sucked in like marijuana smoke, uncovered like the legend of lost and drowned heavenly kingdom of Atlantis, the ancient native south American's tunnels to the underworld, the world under earth's crust where the traveller must shrink on the way down in order to reach the realm where giants still exist – thus accomplished by not eating during the trip for days, weeks etc and never spitted out again like swallowed semen, pills of any kind except in blood.

The atmosphere was turning blue slowly way to quickly as every morn' discomforting need to slough one's skin off in the manner of snakes altering their disguise. Birds screaming at the top of their lungs to hopelessly warn comrades and you futilely, keeping secret restless regrets alive until one runs from invisible without goal alone past mars channels crashing into green dirt to bring forth red pelicans for him to feel even more of an outcast, a loner condemned to be by creation knowing a greater extent than is healthy and productive for getting along with the misery of understanding without being able to act because to early hands got tied and feet shackled but not the mind and so overtaken by oneself, an observer now   – your advantage is what you don't know 'cause it does not bother your soul and thoughts - , outsiders enslaved thrown overboard, looked away carelessly left behind if not jaded enough – it wasn't their fault even though they got told, the ones parading innocence are criminals and will get away with the law they made for themselves, for their selfishness and pretentious they wanna help ya out, they really do, for their own behalf. This horrible machine is too far advanced. Some find a way, some stupidly pray but most of who I am talking about are doomed 'til the end of their days.

Through grey cold deserts chased by still oak galls vomited by the Cynipidae family for coming together dinner. Stray shadow cacti blooming seasonable pursuant all years dry period creeping behind, sneaking laggards bog down in quicksand and the ghosts padding the unlucky with sand grains and holing them brutally with their own ripped off roots. Running, clapping as fast as the twinkling of an eye. Godspeed my love, I hate you.

As the mental boat was coming ashore at foreseen destination Edward Ed or Ed Edward let himself fall into a perfectly placed wicker chair to overview low grounds ruins of obliterated civilizations where shadowed people delivering fey theatre plays 24/7, changing positions with the movement of sun ra and his reflection, hereabout mounts and most important the beige sky. Waiting with a hunting rifle on his lap for pigeons to cross the way to shoot, camouflage bags tied around their necks. Ecstasy! - inside. This route was a smuggling route used by pigeons to smuggle drugs over country borders for creative dealers. Ed used this opportunity often to enjoy the dry air morning turning noon, getting his head free and stock up on stuff. A flickering light beam appeared on top of a hill... seizing curiosity. There he met Jahveh, naked tied to a leafless tree on one of the mountains around in stark wasteland of dreary desolateness. New world science and modern medicine killed culture, society, abandoned him on deserted plateau of dust and stoned replaced by the money god infiltrated and substituted by big companies that are worth not even a wet shit the size the jewels of Goliath. Jahveh he called himself, Jesus he was like Jesse James was a likeness Robin Hood's. Purple dotted veins skinned and scalped sculpture ignited in flames at sundown to shine how the sun does, imitate the way sunflower tries to be but is worshipping down on their knees as a cheap portrayal of the great. But mistress moon's silver coin's brighter than any madman's ideas to get a page in hypocrite press or a weak book for a look and dictates every night's howlin' from lonely rider lone wolf wandering lone lost soul's dances trance glances.

Chemical Reaction. Burned corpse smoking like on grill forgotten steak and leafs of conflagrative.

The man pissing every day at the same afternoon hour in front of his tavern in a puissant spurt like from a garden hose on the inclined alleyway. When folks are passing he kindly pays attention not to wet them. Inevitable it is to walk on the urine soaked stones after the path is turned into a yellow orange idyllic warm creek. Habitual Edward was moving in direction of the running water but winds change and so he found himself in the situation of a salmon and obtained new great wisdom by unwittingly breaking the pattern of rationality and habituality.

It's easy to walk towards lunar, so turn around to the sun.

If one is not inside one is not going to get any insight and as soon as you have a clue what the heck you are doing you are lost.

They are taking everything from you. Your cigarettes, your fake gold wedding ring, sunglasses only worn for purpose of hiding windows to the soul – insecurity, ceramic teeth, they cut out parts of your skin with tattoos to put them in very old precious wooden frames on the wall of their warm sweet homes where they don't have to lift a finger to eat dinner or cut their toenails. They won't stop 'til you are dead. Oh! He's dead anyway. Let us deface him by taking his dirty clothes and let him lay on the raw asphalt in the middle of the street with the dagger still in his half opened face. Conscious. Trying to speak, trying to tell something. Blood streams from gibble gabble begging for help. Only the dead is valuable, that one thing that will come to bring. They won't stop until they have everything but they will have nothing. They didn't stop until you didn't want your own anymore. Give it away. I won't need it today, my heart is displayed, it's getting in my way. Only solution is chaos and the only answer is chaos. Else is senseless fabrication to not become who one is. To stay in line for fucks sake. Stay in line so you'll be fine. And never, never try! Because failing is fun and success is also. In the end we will still be looking into the shaft of a gun.

Burger with crunchy fries and chicken fingers, few beers. Take away – food was good but the place was shit. Little doll companions, wearing knitted pink cardigan along lines scuttling fire ants. A nut from Cocos Islands – the coconut. With a straw milking mother's tit's tastiest ouzo to get on the market for a buck and the reincarnation as a cow in India is the highest aim to achieve as a clueless ignorant bastard. When the when then the then when the then then the when.

Back at his apartment in the organised disorganisation and the disorganised organisation (of the organic organ the organ) to while the time away, spending so much time doing something, so spending too much time doing nothing. Blue last light clouds and miserable evening when Ed heard a voice call his name. Was it just his schizophrenia or was there someone whispering? Did he hallucinate again? Edward looked around but found nobody... It was dark when he got outside. Did it rain? Didn't know such thing. Stood in ajar door of staircase in patio. Cold? No. going through short hallway back to apartment door on ground floor where he lived and this was the reason for invariably drawn curtains and never unclosed windows. Along the walls paintings he himself made were hung up. A lot of them. Painter's hands replaced by brushes and his body liquid was acryl and oil. His productivity was non-stop around the clock. Work described as expressionism. When he wiped his ass there was another work worth thousands and so on. Into burning candles bed-chamber, vinyl rotating soundless. The end. On the chair not able to talk, not able to move, not able to answer, not a centimetre.

Wonderful! Straight on bed. Sensing liquid of blood pumping through heart, heartache, through motionless body. The heart had a hole through which blood expired out of vein and artery inside out. The lung had a hole and filled slowly with fluid, concentration there. More blood at other locations leaking. No movement still. Just lay. Waiting (until it would be over). He should fall asleep as soon as it would work out. Ed kissed her. She kissed him. Did he kiss her? Did she kiss him? Sleeping. She stayed, she left, she was there, she was away.

Wakening.

'I will go now.'
'Where to?'
'Seeking.'
'What will you seek for?'
'I don't know.'
'But what are you hoping to find?'
'I don't know, that's why I'll be seeking.'
'Will you come back?'
'Maybe.'
She was gone.

Isn't love a wonderful magical thing? Female spiders eating their lovers after they have planted the seed of life in them. That's what is called absolute unconditional devotion. Not too different from us – sex is a meal. Butterflies in the stomach and crawling out the expectants mother's vagina – the sign of pre-birth to an unearthly beauty.

At the kitchen table drinkin' whiskey and candle burnin'. Fiddler hat. One naked.

'Put some clothes on.'
One dresses. One is two.
'You wanna play chess?'
'Chess?'
'Let's play chess.'

Edward plays chess, against himself. He loses... shouldn't be drinking so much – destroys brain cells.

'I know.'
'You know?'

'We know.'
'I know I am you.'
'We are us.'
'Are we?'
'You are me.'
'I am myself.'
'Are you sure about that?'
'Right now I am.'
'Because I think you're not.'
'Yes, I'm not.'
'You talk too much.'
Talking too much.
'Well, you don't talk.'
'Thanks.' Mumbling out loud 'I talk to myself sometimes.'
'How is your life going by the way? Haven't seen you for a while.'
'I don't go out. I shun places with a lot of people, makes me nervous. Only existent you are not.'
'I am if you are.'
'People are not what they tell you they are.'

Solitaire - silence.

Edward was spending a lot of time taking baths. But.

What's time. (Question mark). Did not own no clock. He was timeless. Months passed by like trains – fast without anything happening but suddenly to halt and people come and people go and people go and people come without saying hello goodbye and one of them is you.

Half a year. Later.

The amphetamine junkie sitting blank in the apartment on the last chair in one piece left, more chairs comminuted in the tiny kitchen – easily mistaken as contemporary art sculpture - in the middle of the room appearing looking expressionless at his only belongings - a glass vase with an incognizable withered flower. White walls as white as the stuff he used, the film on his tongue and he himself with dark circles around eyes. Could have mistaken him for a plant. Brain must be dried up sitting for days motionless analysing concentrated the searing while sniffing oneself into a statue.

No thoughts.

Couldn't put them into words, the intellect of most human forms doesn't suffice, what a drag. - Physical existence was already not developed enough to memorize and as soon as achieved what does it matter? It's a very weird journey. We do not really need to know all this for now. Life is evanescent but being is endless.

Only three dreams away from reality. Neverending fear the awaiting of awakening.

A drugged woman on h is walking around the block following a car away. On the other side of the river is the desert with mountains and houses. There she gets raped.

Everything is overcast with white smooth bed sheets. The buildings. The asphalt. The sky. It doesn't smell, there is no smell. On heroin for three days and ketamine before or afterwards – retention gone. In between and then again. Met her there in the last previous sentence.

'We were sleeping at the beach.'

On the beach an impressive mutation of man and crab coming straight forward. The sun was shining strong though it wasn't hot. Neither was it cool. All was fine.

'The sky was clear with those stars you call the Milky Way, one less after a supernova like if god took a picture of us. There were strange funnel-shaped light beams separated at the shore – men with flashlights on their heads wandering and when looking down in the water light would shine down their bodies. Were they searching? What were they searching? Nothing. They were fishermen waiting for the fishes from the sea to fish through the whole night on a beach a sweaty day walk away from the village. One leaving only as a shadow near the waves. In the morning they were all gone. Music was to be heard from that lonely house deeper in land up the straight path we came down here. We've already heard those musicians as walking by their ground but decided not to go there. More lights were shining through the trees nearby. The only trees except for those few on the beach.'

Fragments. Left only.

Detoxication station 17.

Marbles splashing on shifting cobblestone, drifting sips and lifting sighs. Breaking down polytoxicant's crushing withdrawal sweat, cold heat, Eastern orthodox. Crashing cymbal dishware.

Kira the lusty voodoo hexed vixen to get rid of her spell to marry ten men in church or mussel. A kiss, on the mouth, another one, one more. – Psychotics - usually they left him alone which was heavily appreciated that way. But was he up for it? Sure he was. She sat on him. On his hard-on naked. Gazing from ilium up her well-shaped corpus. Belly, breasts, neck... Neck? Where the fuck is her face? Where it should have been is a blind spot. One can't look behind it or at where the head could have been severed. Is just nothing. No available visual information. One can't make out with somebody without head but there are sounds, somewhere different. Ed's brain stopped working as if someone had sewn his skull open, taken the brain out and closed it again. That always happened when he's overtasked – no sleep, nothing to eat, dehydrated, stressed etc. Worms and insects hatch out of chrysalises. The sky is full of them. Closing eyes. Did eyes get actively closed? Or were they already before wanting to and doing so? If they were already closed what will be seen when opened if they were already closed? Opened eyes. Black tranquillity. Death is not black. Death is bright and light, radiant and lucid. Death is not quiet, also not loud. Audio is non-existent. And one can't open eyes or close. One is not in possession of eyes. One is. One was. One will always be. Never. So it's not death.

It's rare to find people with their head on their shoulders between their legs.

Optical illusionist translucent womb double trouble. Sky is burning of sun fire.

The immediate second Ed stepped out on the hospital terrace it began to rain. Marvelous! Leaning against the wall he sat down and felt rain growing stronger and lighter on his bare cold hands while listening to raindrops breaking at leaves of vinegar and roof, breathing freshened wet air. As soon as it went away he went away.

Fever – body and mind imploding. Smell of urine.

Amnesia.

i. Roland Barthes, "The Death of the Author," *Image, Music, Text,* Trans. Stephen Heath (New York: Hill and Wang Press, 1977), 146.

ii. Ibid., 147.

iii. Helene Cixous, *Coming to Writing and Other Essays.* Trans. Deborah Jensen (Cambridge: Harvard University Press, 1991), 160.

iv. Amy Shuman, "Gender and Genre," *Feminist Theory and the Study of Folklore,* eds. Susan Tower Hollis, Linda Pershing, M Jane Young (Urbana and Chicago: University of Illinois Press, 1993), 71.

v. Ibid., 71.

vi. Ibid., 72.

vii. Ibid., 72.

viii. Sol Lewitt, "Sentences on Conceptualism," http://www.altx.com/vizarts/ conceptual.html,

ix. I prefer the term "non-rational" to refer to different types of knowledge, because of the connection of irrationality with mental illness. I can think against the grain of "rationality" and not necessarily be "irrational."

x. Cixous, 36.

xi. Deborah Cameron, *The Feminist Critique of Language,* (New York: Routledge, 1998), 8.

xii. In *Gender Trouble,* Judith Butler talks about the moment the declaration is made "It's a girl." Butler tells us, a whole universe of implications is set in motion.

xiii. From a personal conversation with Raymond Norris and also from his Joint Thematic Presentation.

xiv. Cixous, 161.

xv. Ibid., 42.

xvi. Ibid., 41.

Endnotes for Laura Winton's *ECRITURE FEMININE AND WOMEN'S TRANSGRESSIVE WRITING.*

OTHER BOOKS AVAILABLE FROM THRICE PUBLISHING

OUR DOLPHIN – a novella – JOEL ALLEGRETTI

SO WHAT IF IT'S TRUE – LORRI JACKSON

THE HEART CROSSWAYS – JAMES CLAFFEY

Available at

ThricePublishing.com